OTHER BOOKS BY JANE LOUISE CURRY

The Bassumtyte Treasure
Poor Tom's Ghost
The Wolves of Aam
Shadow Dancers
The Great Flood Mystery

Margaret K. McElderry Books

THE
LOTUS
CUP

THE LOTUS CUP

※ ❦ ※

Jane Louise Curry

A Margaret K. McElderry Book

Atheneum   1986   New York

Library of Congress Cataloging-in-Publication Data

Curry, Jane Louise.
The Lotus cup.

"A Margaret K. McElderry book."
Summary: Though two boys are paying attention to her,
a seventeen-year-old in East Liverpool, Ohio, is
painfully shy until she discovers in herself the eye,
hand, and heart of a potter.
[1. Pottery—Fiction.   2. East Liverpool (Ohio)—
Fiction]   I. Title.
PZ7.C936Lot   1986   [Fic]   85-21467
ISBN 0-689-50384-9

WITH THANKS TO H.B.
AND EVERYONE IN TOWN
WHO HELPED

THE
LOTUS
CUP

One

ORRY TIPSON WATCHED the snow fall from the shelter of the high school's entryway.

Two days into spring and it was snowing. Again.

Small, with red-blonde hair more frizzy than curly, and wearing over her pink shirt a shapeless green sweater so oddly long that it hung halfway to the hem of her pink-and-yellow skirt, Corry stood with her bookbag between her feet and clipped on the shiny plastic earrings that tinkled too much to wear in class. She buttoned up her baggy tweed coat and took her time looping the long, knitted muffler around the turned-up collar. She adjusted her earmuffs. By the time she had pulled on her purple knitted gloves, most of the other students in her Art Appreciation class had vanished down the steps toward the lower parking area. The boys who couldn't cram themselves into Angie Dalla's car would be riding with Jim George, or with Gail and the others in Moby Dick, Scott Gassler's lumbering old white Chevy.

As she pushed out through the middle door, Corry bent over with a stomach pang even worse than the last. *It's all in your head. Ignore it,* she told herself fiercely as she straightened and threaded her way through the faculty parking lot toward the little group by Mrs. Giorgiadis's station wagon. It couldn't be indigestion from lunch. Not from cottage cheese and Jell-O. It was just plain old misery, a tight discomfort that every once in a while gave a squeeze that left her breathless. Could algebra give you an ulcer? She had thought that the quiz fourth period was going really well until, half finished, she looked at the clock. Five minutes to go. She had done it again.

"Corry? Hurry it up!" Mrs. Giorgiadis called, her breath frosting out in the snowy air. She stood holding the collar of her puffy quilted coat up around her ears, looking like a roly-poly cartoon of herself. At Corry's approach, she brushed the snow from her dark curls and bundled herself into the driver's seat, calling out the window as Corry reached the car.

"Other side, up front. You'll have to sit on Linda's lap. I think the seat's back far enough for the safety belt to reach around the both of you."

It was a tight squeeze. When, after an awkward struggle, the belt's buckle snicked fast, its strap cut right across Corry's uneasy middle.

Mrs. Giorgiadis frowned as she turned the ignition

4

key. "Are you all right, Corry? You look a little green around the gills."

Corry made a face. "Indigestion. I'll be OK."

"You must've had macaroni and cheese for lunch, too." Kim Long, in the back seat, giggled. "It's usually pretty good, but I think I hit the bottom of the pot. Mrs. Bissell could hardly shake it off the serving spoon. It looked like lumpy orangey library paste. I couldn't finish it."

"I was so famished, I ate all of mine," Sue Letterman said. "I can still feel it rumbling around down there. There's this big, pale orange lump in a puddle of milk and Coke."

"You're a great help," Mrs. Giorgiadis said drily. "Any more and we'll *all* be sick before we reach the museum. How about another subject?"

As the station wagon made its cautious way down the St. Clair Avenue hill into the town sheltering between the high-shouldered hills and the Ohio River, Corry closed her eyes. Long practice made it easy to shut out the chatter about Friday's baseball game in Wellsville, the wild velvet jacket Jack Crossland had worn to Angie Dalla's birthday party, and whether *merde!* counted as a dirty word when you weren't in France or with somebody French. Withdrawing into herself, she began the old, calming litany. *The test's over, Tipson. Done. Finished.*

There was nothing to be done about it now, she told herself. Save the worrying for beforehand. After all, it wasn't as if she didn't under*stand* powers and roots. She did. She really did. And she *could* be faster. The test only meant

5

she needed more practice. Do the homework twice over. That would help. And things wouldn't be half so bad if only—Corry drew a deep breath—if only her mother didn't always make such an unholy scene.

By the time the station wagon angled back into the last vacant parking space along the side of the State Store, Corry felt enough better to snatch a quick look in the mirror on the backside of the windshield visor and hastily repair her lipstick while Linda Bass struggled to unfasten the safety belt. To her dismay, the silvery pink that matched her earrings made her look even paler than she felt. She rubbed most of it off again.

The Moby Dick was parked just ahead, and its passengers, except for Gail Mestrovic, were already halfway down the block toward the dignified old building that had once been the post office, but now housed the Museum of Ceramics. Gail, as tall and dark as Corry was small and strawberry-fair, was waiting on the corner. She drew Corry aside as Linda and the others crossed the street.

"Did you ask him?"

"Ask who?" Corry said blankly.

"Don, for Pete's sake. You were going to ask him at lunch. About going to the movies Friday night."

"Oh. No, I didn't need to ask. I heard him tell Bob Wainer he was going to Wellsville to cover the game for the *Keramos*." The *Keramos* was the school paper. And it was just as well Don was going. The game might keep his mind off Angie Dalla, who'd turned him down the last two times he'd asked her out. At a boy-gets-girl movie like *The Drama Club*, he would end up feeling sorrier for himself than ever. Poor Don! He and his kid sisters and brothers lived across Fourth Street from Corry, and he had been her friend since the first grade. She had been *really* shy back then—too shy even to respond to their teacher's questions. For weeks she had whispered her answers to Don, who announced them to Miss McGrory with a confidence Corry still envied. Whether that cheerful confidence would survive Angie Dalla, she wasn't sure.

"Well, then," Gail said briskly. "What about the new guy? Tip what's-his-name. Meredith? I see him watching you sometimes in class. Why not ask him? Scott can give him a ride home in Moby Dick if he needs it. I think he lives somewhere on up past the cemetery."

"Maybe," Corry said. But she knew she wouldn't. Asking Don Chappick to the movies would feel like asking a brother or a cousin, but Tip Meredith was a stranger. And not very friendly. He had transferred to East Liverpool High School at the beginning of March from somewhere in New England and was still keeping himself to himself.

"I'll think about it," she said.

Pushing through the double glass doors of the museum, Corry followed Gail as she threaded her way through the knot of students shedding hats and coats and mufflers. Those who, like Corry, had never been in the museum before were looking around curiously at the marble floors, tall pilasters, and elaborate arched ceiling. As Corry moved on past, Don Chappick, a lanky, freckled redhead, put a hand on her shoulder.

"Hi." Corry managed a smile. "Where do we put our coats?"

7

"Over there." Don indicated a coatrack beyond a nearby display case, and then frowned down at her. "You OK?"

"Just a headache," Corry lied. "No big deal."

In the museum's auditorium, Tip Meredith climbed up to the top level and chose the folding chair next to Corry's. "Hi," he said offhandedly.

"Hi." Corry smiled briefly.

Tip was tall and dark-haired and behind his glasses had nice, dark eyes, but he had made no friends in the weeks since he had enrolled at the high school. He never had much to say, even in class, but for a moment Corry thought he was about to speak. She was relieved when he leaned forward, elbows on his knees, to wait for the orientation slide show to begin. As the lights went down, Corry closed her eyes gratefully and leaned her head back against the wall. Her stomach had settled down to a dull tightness. By the time she walked the six or so blocks home and had something to eat, it would be all right. *Everything* would be all right if her mother weren't dead set on her going to college. No more algebra. No geometry or chemistry senior year. Instead, she could be taking Foods I and II—and next year maybe art again, instead of French.

As the lights went down and orchestral music filled the little auditorium, Corry tried to concentrate on breathing deeply. It helped sometimes. When a narrator's smooth voice took the music's place, she tried to tune it out. For a while it worked. The voice slid unheard through her mind

8

until it said . . . *of clay and water, much in the fashion of decorating a birthday cake.* . . .

Corry, her attention caught, opened her eyes, but whatever it had been was gone. Old views, advertisements, posters and pottery pieces alternated on the screen almost magically, as if several projectors were working at once. She watched halfheartedly as the images came and went.

. . . *By 1900 forty-five percent of the general ceramic ware in the United States came from East Liverpool.* . . .

Corry blinked. *Forty-five* percent? Then, as yet another slide of chinaware flashed on the screen, she leaned forward, suddenly wide awake. Two pieces, a white, narrow-necked pitcher and a lidded bowl unlike anything she had ever seen before, caught her eye and then were gone. The bowl might have been a bowl in a fairy tale. Its filigree ornamentation was as rich and elaborate as if the bowl were encrusted with pearls. A few spots were touched with jewel-like color. It might have been a master pastry-cook's masterpiece. A splendid orb to crown a royal wedding cake.

Corry, stomach-ache forgotten, watched the rest of the slides avidly, hoping to see more such pieces. But the show had turned into a portrait of the town in the 1890s, with photographs of picnics, sports teams, the senior class of '97, proud pottery workers, bustling streets, the roller coaster at vanished Rock Springs Park, and handsome unfamiliar buildings. The Keystone-Cops uniforms of the tiny police force brought a laugh, but with the account of the decline of the potteries, the mood of the audience sobered.

The end was at hand, the narrator intoned. Corry felt

9

an odd mixture of grief and pride as she watched the images of energy and prosperity give way to failure, the Depression, and demolition as the good times became, in the narrator's conclusion, "a sad memory, fixed in time."

As the screen darkened, a light went on in a small display shelf set into the wall to its left, and then winked off as another near it was illuminated. Others appeared one by one nearby, below the screen and in the right-hand wall, each showing yet another handsome bowl or pitcher or cup. In one, the wonderful bowl itself appeared and then vanished.

When the auditorium lights came up at last, Corry heard Tip Meredith draw in his breath. "Fan*tas*tic." He straightened from his hunched-over position, stretched, and slumped back against the wall. "*Encore!*" he whispered, and Corry, darting a sideways look, saw that he was off in some world of his own.

A scattering of the students applauded. Tike Persons, down front, drummed his feet and boomed, "Cartoon! Where's the cartoon?" A high-pitched voice squeaked an answer from somewhere in the back, "In the front row!" and at that everyone cheered.

Mrs. Giorgiadis moved to the doorway and held up a hand. "If you'll all follow me, please, I want to point out a few things in one or two of the displays outside. Then you're on your own. There are life-size dioramas downstairs that will give you some idea of what working in a pottery was like in the so-called 'good old days,' and the display cases in the rear gallery show pieces from a number of the local potteries."

Corry, her stomach-ache forgotten, snatched up her bookbag and hurried down across the stepped seating area, making straight for the bowl that looked so eerily like glossy sugar icing. *Covered Lotus Ware rose jar—Knowles, Taylor & Knowles, circa 1895,* the card read. Even close up, the jar looked like a pastry-cook's fantasy in Royal Icing—or would have, except for the glaze's sheen and the hint of translucence. The delicate filigree, its scrollwork made even more elaborate by the addition of beading, stood out from the body of the bowl like heavy lace. Even the fanciest icing-lace patterns in her mother's *Encyclopedia of Cake Decoration,* Corry decided, would look tacky beside it.

She leaned her forehead against the glass. Suppose—If this looked so much like icing, why couldn't cake frosting be made to look like this? It would be difficult to draw, but with a picture, the next time she helped her mother with one of her wedding-cake orders, she could give it a try. It would make a fantastic top tier, and instead of shell borders around the lower tiers, she could do bands of beading like the two around the bowl's lid.

"Corry?" Gail looked in at the doorway just as the lights went out. "What are you lurking in the dark for? Mrs. G. says get your buns out here."

"I think I put it a little more politely than that," Mrs. Giorgiadis drawled, appearing behind her.

Gail turned, blushing, but passed it off with a grin.

"Sorry about that."

Mrs. Giorgiadis spoke to the class briefly about the elements that could make the design of one piece "classic" and others hopelessly dated. In one display case she pointed

11

out the simplicity of design in a white tea set made in 1875, in an 1879 ironstone pitcher, and an ivory cup and saucer made in 1895 that would make any of them perfectly at home on a present-day table.

"But *not* the plate to the right," she observed. "It's beautifully made, the gold on brown-lustre border is handsome, but the young woman in medieval costume not only has an 1890s hairdo, but takes the design across the line between 'elaborate' and 'overdone.' She's high-class 'kitsch.' Now, the red doughnut-shaped teapot down here is dated, too." She pointed. "It almost shouts 'Circa 1940!' but it's amusing, so some of us might still be happy to have one."

Linda Bass stretched up to peer at the ivory cup and saucer. "Gosh, look at how beautiful the decoration around the rim is. When you see the blah new dishes my mom just got, it seems weird this was made on the same *planet*. But ours are from the same company."

Mrs. Giorgiadis nodded. "Don't quote me, but as I understand it, back in the thirties when the potteries that survived the '29 crash realized how fast the Japanese were gaining on them, they concentrated on trying to compete for the mass market—the 'everyday' china and hotelware—and it's hard to attract top-notch designers for that sort of thing. A really good designer in *any* of the arts wants to work toward his or her vision of the best, not toward the lowest common denominator. The Japanese caught on fast and managed to combine acceptable designs with their far cheaper labor costs. Lenox China, the British, and to some degree the Germans and Scandinavians, have kept the top of the market, and left us—"

"Sitting on our keesters," Lew Dixter volunteered.

Don Chappick made a mournful face. "I never thought I'd get depressed over *dishes.*"

"It's no joke. It *is* depressing," Tip Meredith cut in sharply. "Some of these old pieces are incredibly good. Doesn't it make anybody—well, *angry* that it's all over?"

There was a startled silence.

"Cheer up." Mrs. Giorgiadis said easily. "Not *all* is lost. You know the Norman Rockwell collectors' pieces— not the ones in supermarkets, but the good Gorham ones you see advertised in magazines? Homer Laughlin Company makes the blanks for the cups and mugs. It may not make them a threat to Lenox China, but it is a step back up in the world."

She looked at her watch. "All right, you're on your own. You have half an hour before they throw us out."

Corry drifted back around the gallery, looking for more of the filigreed Lotus Ware, but found none. She vaguely remembered having seen a stairwell on the other side of the main entrance and went in search of it. Passing a case displaying an elegant seven-piece Victorian boudoir set that included a washbowl, pitcher, and lidded chamber pot and slop jar, she heard Tike Persons snort in disbelief. "You're having me on. It'd be like sitting on a fancy flower-pot." Corry stifled a grin. Trust Tike to find the bathroom crockery.

Downstairs, Corry—who had wondered briefly what a "diorama" was when Mrs. Giorgiadis mentioned it—walked into what, for a flicker of a moment, appeared to be a clay-

13

grimed, brick-walled workroom where two boys and a man and woman silently labored to fill the tall shelf rack of bowls nearby. Then she saw that the flat pancake of clay the first boy held in mid-air would never slap down on the plaster form, that the workman holding the template never turned his half-shaped bowl, and that the clay-colored water from the sponge held by the weary-looking young woman smoothing bowl rims ran down the sides of her little turntable in motionless drips. They were mannequins, wonderfully, eerily realistic. Further along, on the right, two workmen were shown stacking a kiln with ceramic containers—"saggers," the explanation boards along the railing called them—full of plates and bowls and saucers.

At the sudden clatter of feet on the stairs and exclamations behind her of "Hey, look at this!" and "Where's Angie?" Corry moved quickly into the next room, which turned out to be the decorating shop. Here too the workers' clothing and the women's hairdos suggested the 1890s. Wooden trays of glazed plates and cups waited for the man seated at a small decorating turntable to line their rims with gold. A spectacled woman looked up thoughtfully from her sheet of decals—probably wondering why she had cut into the middle of the sheet rather than starting at the edge—and a pensive young woman hesitated before stamping the pottery's mark on the bottom of a dinner soup bowl.

"This is where I'd work," Corry whispered to herself, caught in the illusion. But no decals. She would paint fine plates or pieces like the pitcher atop the man's work shelves with lush roses, and embellish them with gold. Decorating a four-tier wedding cake might be more fun, but what did you have to show for it after the wedding? Crumbs!

Past an almost life-sized photo-mural of a group of 1896 pottery workers, Corry found the main display room. Tall glass cases ranged along the walls and in rows like library shelves displayed the wares of long-vanished potteries, of others swallowed up in later companies, and of the few that still survived.

More Lotus Ware, labeled Knowles, Taylor and Knowles, and dated "circa 1895," was displayed on three shelves of the case directly ahead. There was a scallop-edged candy dish with leaflike veining that stood on feet like bits of twig, and a beautiful wide translucent bowl like a swirl of seashell but, to Corry's disappointment, none of the wedding-cake filigree work.

On a shelf nearby, though, a hexagonal peach-colored plate with a fine raised rim and what looked like ivory peachblossom petals wind-scattered across its face caught her eye. *Pelican Pottery, 1927–1931,* the placard said. Her Grandfather Tipson had had something to do with the Pelican Pottery. What, she wasn't sure. He had died just before Corry's father was born, and all her mother seemed to know about him was that he had been a very unhappy man. From the way she said it, Corry suspected that it meant he drank too much. The photograph on the placard showed a secretaryish-looking woman, a gentleman in a hat, and thirty or so workmen standing in front of a door in a brick wall.

15

The name *Tipson* suddenly sprang out at her from the paragraph below the photograph: *The Pelican Pottery, formerly a department of Tipson and Son, became an independent division in 1927 when that company reorganized. Under John Tipson's management, and after 1929 under his ownership, Pelican concentrated on the production of fine dinnerware, but the firm was crippled by the 1929 stock market crash. It closed its doors in 1931.*

Corry stared. Her grandpa's *own* pottery? One that had been part of an even bigger Tipson company? But that couldn't be right. Could it? Neither her mother nor Grandma Binney had ever said Word One about any Tipsons ever *owning* a pottery. But—there weren't any other Tipsons in town, so who else could it be? If she counted her mother as a Binney, Corry herself was The Last of the Tipsons.

Tipson and Son. . . . There must be a Tipson and Son display too. Corry made her way eagerly up one aisle and down the next, peering over shoulders when other members of the class stood in the way, and bending down every few steps to check the lower shelves. She found it at last in one of the cases along the wall just as Tip Meredith, who had been bending down to read the placard, moved away. Flanked by a rose-bordered plate and a flower vase with a raised design of lilies, the placard bore the headings *Tipson and Perry Pottery (1893–1905)* and *Tipson and Son (1905–1927)*. A photograph of a stern, stiff-collared young man was captioned *Lucas Henry Tipson.*

Corry skimmed through the two short paragraphs and then reread them carefully, little wiser than before. There was no explanation why the company had been broken up in 1927, only the bare fact. But if the John Tipson of the Pelican Pottery *was* her grandfather, that would make the handsome but rather forbidding Lucas Tipson—a potter originally from Staffordshire in England—her great-grandfather. He looked a little—just a little—like photographs of her own father, who had died in a road accident when she was six. But her father, whom everyone had loved but who failed at everything he tried, could never have had that cool "I am Somebody" look.

Corry hugged herself with pleasure, as if that aura of somebodyness had reached out to surround the red-gold hair and thin, eager face reflected in the glass of the case. Then she hurried back to read the account of the Pelican Pottery again. When the room began to empty, Corry reluctantly followed the others. She would just have to come back, even if it *did* cost more when you didn't come with a class. And her mother, on her next Thursday off—she'd have to come, too.

Near the gallery entrance Tip Meredith, who stood frowning at the photo mural, turned to stare at Corry. She felt her cheeks redden and tried to hide her confusion behind a vague smile as she moved past.

His hand shot out so quickly to grasp her arm that Corry, caught off balance, stumbled as she was swung around to face the proud, stiff faces of the pottery workers in the old photograph.

"Hey, what—Let go, will you!" Corry protested.

"No, *look*," he said intently. "The girl in the checked blouse. Don't you see?"

"What *is* it, Mouse?" Tike Persons loomed up behind them. He didn't like "that Meredith jerk," and couldn't remember ever hearing Corry speak so sharply. Linda Bass, Kim Long, and several others slowed on their way out to the stairs.

Corry wrenched her arm away. "Nothing," she said in confusion at finding herself the center of attention.

Tip Meredith seemed oblivious to the general hostility. "Don't you see the resemblance?" he insisted. He turned impatiently from Corry to the others. "There, in the second row. Look at the girl on the left, in the checked blouse. And now look—"

To Corry's astonishment—and embarrassment—he reached out to pull her long hair back, away from her face, and up, twisting it into an untidy topknot.

"There!"

"Hey!" Tike exclaimed, forgetting how satisfying it would have been to punch out the smug, standoffish Meredith. "It is! It's *you,* Mouse."

"That's *weird,*" Linda breathed.

Corry stared. There, facing her from the end of the row of girls and young women was—except for the shabby blouse—a mirror-image of herself. There was the same frizzle of fair curls over the same sharply-arched eyebrows and wide dark eyes. And there were other resemblances. Corry's lace-up boots were neatly polished and the skirt she had made from a length of window-curtain out of a trunk in the Tipson attic was patterned with pink and yellow zigzags, but they were much the same style as the dusty boots and dark skirt worn by the long-ago girl. The only differ-

18

ence between the two girls that anyone could have put a finger on was the proud tilt to the other's firm little chin. Corry would have been looking up shyly through her lashes.

Tip let her hair fall, and shrugged. He seemed to have regained his cool. "Who is she? Your great-granny?" he asked lightly.

"I don't know." For a moment she almost flared out at him, standing there so crisply shirted and confident, probably laughing behind that bored face of his at the long-dead girl's shabby clothing and dusty, cracked boots. "I've got to go."

She hurried out and up the stairs in search of Gail, and the others trailed behind.

All but Tip. He stood for a long moment before the photograph, as if it puzzled him—and then reached out gently to touch the cheek of the girl in the checked blouse.

Two

ORRY PULLED HER key from the lock and stepped into the house, slamming the door shut against the snowy air. She hung her coat and muffler beside the mirror on the old-fashioned wall rack and then slung her bookbag back over her shoulder.

The mail—the phone bill and a GREATEST SPRING SALE EVER hardware-store advertisement—lay on the hall table. Old Mr. Hankins in the apartment upstairs might not be able to take his daily walks with the sidewalks snowed up again, but he never failed to make it down to check the mail. Corry always wondered why he bothered. The Hankinses never got anything but bills and throwaways. She knew that because in the summer she always made it to the mailbox first. The two of them were as quiet as little mice up there, and just about as shy, so if it weren't for the mail being on the hall table instead of in the mailbox, you'd never know they were OK.

The hallway was *cold*. Corry headed back past the stairs and through the swinging door into the kitchen. Dropping her bookbag and gloves on the table, she made straight for the old-fashioned gas range, took down the kitchen matches and—being very careful since the *phloom!* of the igniting gas always made her nervous—lit the oven. Then, unlocking the cellar door—which was kept locked because the outside cellar door was falling apart and couldn't keep out a cat, let alone a prowler—she went down to stoke up the furnace. She was supposed to put on only one or two shovelsful of coal at a time during the daytime but, thinking of the Hankinses, she slung in a third. Last night, out in the back shed where kerosene for the space heater was kept, she had noticed that only one of the five-gallon plastic cans marked *H* had any fuel in it. Mr. H. usually paid Don Chappick to get the first container filled as soon as it was empty, so that there was always a spare. Corry had meant to ask Mr. H. about it, but forgot. It was easy enough to keep a kitchen warm, but without a heater to warm it up before bedtime, a bedroom was only one notch up from an igloo.

Back upstairs, Corry pulled one of the tall kitchen stools to the end of the table nearest the warmth of the oven and got out her algebra book and notebook. The stool was uncomfortable, but no chair was high enough for the long, wide worktable. Like the Tipson house itself, the table dated back to the 1890s, when cooking for family

21

meals was a much more important and complicated business, and kitchens were as large as living rooms. Lucas Henry Tipson. Of course . . . *he* must have built the house. The dates were right, and once upon a time the house *had* been really nice. Not even the peeling paint and sagging porch steps could hide that.

Maybe Lucas Henry and Great-Grandma even had a cook. After all, take out the plasterboard partition that divided Corry's own bedroom from her mother's, and you would have the original dining room, a room long enough for twenty people to sit down to dinner—if you had a table long enough. And Great-Grandfather Stiff-Collar would have had. . . .

Corry hadn't felt at all like settling down to algebra but by 6:30, when she heard the front storm door's bang, she had completed the assignment and was halfway through the same material a second time. Hurriedly, she shoved the algebra work into the bookbag and pulled out her English book, then dashed to the refrigerator. From the freezer compartment she took a box of fish sticks and a half-full bag of French fries, spread them out on a cookie sheet, and was sliding the sheet into the oven as her mother, laden down with two bulging plastic shopping bags, bumped the swinging door open.

"Quick!" April Tipson moaned. "Take this one before my fingers break off. I think they're frozen stiff. Ooh, that's better. Thanks, honey. I thought a couple of times me and the groceries were gonna end up all over the sidewalk. It's really slippy out there."

She went back out to hang up her coat and scarf and returned to stand rubbing her hands while Corry unloaded the bags onto the table and put the eggs, lemons, and cartons of milk and cream in the refrigerator. A pretty, faded blonde with a short mop of curls, shrewd blue eyes and a cheery, outgoing manner, she was the same height as Corry but seemed even shorter because of her plumpness. She filled out her supermarket-checker's uniform generously.

"Leave the powdered sugar out, and one of the lemons, hon. I have to start on the decorations for the Oakleys's cake tonight. The sooner we eat, the better."

"I've got fish and French fries in the oven, but I only just put them in." Corry moved her books and papers to the far end of the table. "Why tonight instead of tomorrow? I thought their party wasn't until Saturday."

Her mother crossed to the cutlery drawer and took out knives and forks. "It's a big party—for about ninety—so the cake's got to be two tiers. And the icing stethoscope I was going to make to decorate the top is out. Mrs. Oakley phoned this morning before I left for work. Now it's to celebrate more than their son's finishing his—what's it called? internship? He's been invited to join some gold-plated doctor's group in Pittsburgh."

Corry giggled. "She said that? 'Gold-plated'?"

"Well, no. But you can bet your boots that's what she meant. Anyhow, the cake's still to be chocolate, with chocolate icing, but now she wants it to say 'On Top of the World!' and have something real special on top."

"Like what?"

Mrs. Tipson turned on the burner under the teakettle.

23

"Who knows? I thought maybe a little globe up on the top. I could cut one out of cake and ice it and, you know, support it with one of the thin dowels right down through. But then I decided that would look pretty clunky. Any ideas?"

Corry stood for a moment with the paper napkins in her hand, then dropped them on the table and went to root in her bookbag.

"Maybe. Our art class went to the museum this afternoon, remember? Look at this." She handed her mother the postcard she had bought from the rack at the bookstall after her return to the museum's main floor.

The color photograph showed a richly filigreed white Lotus Ware jar, a delicate ewer-shaped jug, also with filigree decoration, and a menu-card holder of the sort once used for formal dinner parties—a holder that looked almost as if it were made of white coral.

"Gosh, they're beautiful!"

"So's the museum. You've got to see it," Corry said enthusiastically. "It's the neatest place I've ever been. And do you know what? They've got this display of Pelican Pottery pieces and it says Grandpa Tipson didn't just work there. He *owned* it. How's come you never told me?"

Her mother shrugged. "I guess I never thought it was any big deal. It was long gone when my folks moved here, and when your dad bragged on it, I never paid much mind. He was the sweetest man in the world, but he always did talk things up."

"Did he ever say anything about Great-Grandpa owning a pottery too? His name was Lucas Henry Tipson, and there's a picture of him in the museum."

"You're kidding! Honest? All your dad ever said was that *his* daddy had some kind of row with the old man. For all I know, your grandma never told him anything more than that. Your granddad died a couple months before your dad was born, and he got the idea his mom somehow held that against your old Lucas Tipson."

"Why? What did Grandpa die of?" Corry ventured. She had never had the nerve before to ask straight out.

"Drink," her mother said flatly. She turned the Lotus Ware postcard over to read the caption.

"I see what you mean about this stuff. It says here the decoration was put on with a tool like a pastry tube." She considered for a moment. "White decorations would sure look nice on the whipped chocolate icing, but I don't see how we could do anything like this, honey. The open-work on these here is stuck on a hollow base—the jar and the jug. There's no way you could make a hollow icing globe, and a solid one would be heavy as a baseball."

Corry hesitated, taking the postcard as her mother handed it back. Then she spied, right under her thumb, what looked like the answer.

"Mom? Look at this holder-thing. The little coral branches are stuck onto a kind of latticework. And a globe has a latticework anyhow—all those latitude and longitude lines. I can at least *try,* can't I?"

"Sure, but how?" Mrs. Tipson opened the oven a crack to peer in. "What'll you use to support it? You can't ice thin air."

Corry grinned. "Remember those Christmas ornaments I made in sixth grade out of string and plaster of Paris and balloons? When the plaster's dry, you untie the balloon and pull it out, and there's this lacy globe. Why couldn't we do that with a really strong icing instead of plaster and string?"

Her mother laughed. "C'mon, Corry! How could you fasten a balloon on the turntable so's you can pipe the icing on? How could you hold it steady? Besides, where'll you get a balloon this time of day? Rayl's is open, but they won't have balloons."

"There's the one I got at Gail's birthday party." It was a long one, purple with *Happy Birthday* written along it, and after having been moored to Corry's bed-post for six weeks, it had begun to shrink. "It's not long for this world anyway."

Mrs. Tipson shrugged. "OK. Give it a try. And I guess if I'm gonna do acorns and oak leaves like Mrs. Oakley wants for around the base, they need to be white too." Mrs. Tipson put the plates by the vent on top of the stove where the oven's heat could warm them. "But you've got to finish your homework first. Let's see, now. We better have a salad."

For as long as Corry could remember, her mother had passed off her questions about her father with vague answers or praise of his sweetness, his thoughtfulness—or even with out-of-the-blue flashes or temper. Now, Corry thought as she finished her last fish stick, the question about Grandpa Tipson had seemed to rub her the wrong way too. But she *had* to know more.

She dipped a forkful of french fries into the catsup at the side of her plate and just before she put them in her mouth said, as if it were only a passing thought, "There was this really weird thing happened at the museum."

"Well—what?" her mother asked after a moment.

Corry pointed to her full mouth, and when she finally swallowed said, "Well. Downstairs, there was this big photo on the wall, like a mural, almost life-size, of some pottery workers back in the 1890s. And there's this girl in it who looks just like me. Everybody said so. It was creepy. I wondered who she was, but I don't know how to find out."

Mrs. Tipson shrugged. "Beats me. I guess she could be a relative. Your Grandma Tipson told your dad his folks on both sides came over from England back in the 1800s to work in the potteries. That's all I ever heard about it."

"Would Granny Binney know?"

"Mom? No, her and Dad only came here in '65. Your Grandma Tipson died in '67—the year before your dad and me got married. Mom never met her. *I* never met her."

Her voice had that flat note in it again, so Corry changed the subject. "There's still some sherbet left. Can we have that?"

Concentration was Corry's strong point. At 9:30, when she put her books away, she was surprised to find that her mother had finished and gone to bed. Without remembering to quiz her on how the algebra quiz had gone! A note on the table said *Rember furnase before you go to bed.* Rember. Remember? Her mother wasn't the world's best speller.

Eighteen perfect small white acorns and three dozen

lifelike small oak leaves lay drying on a sheet of waxed paper beside a covered plastic container and the rolling pin. The sugar, special gelatin, and bottles of gum tragacanth and glycerine had been put away, but the plastic box held a lump of left-over candy ceramic icing in a plastic bag. Another box, in the refrigerator, contained a full batch of extra-strong royal icing. Corry went to get the balloon.

Latticework. It *would* be hard to pipe onto a balloon. You could get away with latticework that was a bit squiggly if you were going to cover it with roses, but not when it was latitude and longitude. But if the lines would be too squiggly with royal icing and the pastry tube, that left only ceramic icing, which dried almost as fast as you could say "Mxyzptlk." Corry scowled as she tied the end of the balloon off into a three-inch globe, but then she brightened and went in search of the noodle cutter.

Once everything she needed was in place, Corry went happily to work, first greasing the large marble work-slab lightly and dusting it with cornstarch, then cutting off a walnut-sized piece of the "ceramic" icing. She had never given a thought to its name before, but now it seemed both funny and fitting. Sealing the rest back up in its container, she rolled the knob of icing out into a long ribbon. This she sliced into narrow strips with one sweep of the pasta cutter's four roller-blades. Then, by moving the cutter an eighth of an inch, she cut the five strips into ten. Working rapidly, she peeled each strip from the marble surface, smoothed it by rolling it lightly back and forth, and put it with the others under a sheet of plastic wrap.

The balloon was almost a bust. A length of paper cut

from a grocery bag and taped tightly around the tail of the once-long balloon made an excellent handle for the purple globe, but then everything seemed to go wrong. At first the thin candy strips stuck to the rubber wherever they happened to touch it, and made the balloon *blip!* in protest when they were pulled off. After several moments' frustration, Corry tried rubbing on a light coating of the glycerine her mother applied to the plastic leaves she used as patterns, but then the longitude, which had to go on first, refused to stay in place even when stuck on at the North and South Poles with a dab of the stickier royal icing. Under the weight of the next-added line or two of longitude, the Poles slid slowly askew, heading for the equator—or where the equator ought to be.

In the end she had to prop the balloon-world on its side and hold the Poles in place with one hand while adding fresh lines with the other. Once a third of the lines had been applied, she began cutting and fixing in place the short lengths which would, as equator and lines of latitude, fasten the longitudinal lines together into a strong framework.

It was not an easy one-hand job, and before the first third was finished, the supply of candy lines waiting under the plastic wrap had grown stiff. By the time Corry cut a second batch, her earlier work was already hard, and not so ticklish to handle. The more she completed, the more quickly the work went. At half past eleven the latticed globe was finished, drying on the waxed paper beside the acorns and oak leaves, and Corry was bent over a sheet of notepaper, trying to remember the shapes of China, and the countries from the eastern end of the Mediterranean to India. Her

North and South America were fine and Africa was not too bad, but Europe's coasts looked somehow wrong, and the Middle and Far East were hopeless. There was a map in her World History book, but that was in her locker at school.

The swinging door creaked open and Mrs. Tipson stood in the doorway in her bathrobe, shading her eyes against the strong light with what appeared to be a small picture frame.

"For Pete's sake, Corry! You have to get up at six-thirty if you're gonna shovel the sidewalk before you catch the school bus."

Corry pushed the paper and pencil away. She would just have to wait until she got to school to do a pattern for the map.

Her mother spied the icing globe and bent close to examine it. "I see it worked after all. Not bad. *If* it holds together after you get the balloon out. *If* you get the balloon out."

"Thanks." Corry made a face. "What have you got there? That's Daddy's picture, isn't it?

"Oh, yeah. I forgot. That's what I got up for. I was having this dream about back when I put it in this old frame ten, maybe twelve years ago, and I remember thinking 'If I don't wake up and look at it now, I'll forget.'" She laid the old silver frame flat on the table, slid the backing free, and drew from under it two photographs, both old, that Corry had never seen before.

"The last time I saw these," Mrs. Tipson said, "you were just a little kid. Here—the first one's your Grandma Tipson. But look at the other one."

The first photograph showed a young woman with short, wavy hair and a pleasant, pretty face. The second, an oval mounted on dark gray cardboard, seemed to be a wedding photograph. A youngish man in formal attire stood beside a seated young woman richly dressed in white silk taffeta with sleeves and bodice embroidered with tiny seed pearls, and wearing a pearl tiara. The young woman was the pottery girl of the checked blouse and dusty boots.

"It's her! The one I saw in the Museum!"

Her mother took the photograph and held it up beside Corry's face. "You sure are like her. It *is* almost spooky."

Corry's eyes shone. "She is my great-grandma, then. Just like Ti—like the kids guessed."

"I don't know, honey. She might be a—a great-great aunt or something."

"No," Corry said positively. She pointed. "That's him. That's Lucas Henry Tipson."

After getting up early to braid a lock of her hair in an elaborate pattern with pink and green ribbons that matched the almost-new man's Hawaiian shirt that had been her best attic find of all, after ironing the shirt, belting it tightly over her black skirt, and planning what she would say when she saw Tip Meredith, Corry was almost too nervous to eat breakfast.

Twice between morning classes Corry tried to get up the nerve to talk to Tip. She finally managed it, hurrying to catch up after he passed in the hall on his way out of the cafeteria after lunch.

"Hi," she said quickly. The words tumbled out in a

rush as she thrust the photograph at him. "I thought you might be interested in this. She *was* my great-grandmother. And that's my great-grandfather, Lucas Henry Tipson."

Tip stopped dead, and the lunchtime traffic flowed around them. He stared at the photograph.

"That's impossible," he said slowly. "Lucas Henry Tipson was *my* great-grandfather. And that's not Great-Grandmother."

Three

"**T**IP" WAS FOR TIPSON? *Lucas Tipson* Meredith? Corry, astonished and half disbelieving, barely made it to her seat in Mr. Harmill's Algebra II class before the bell. She folded her homework assignment, wrote her name on the front, passed it forward and opened her book to the chapter on "Systems of Linear Sentences," all in a daze.

It was true. He had shown her his Connecticut driver's license. So he must be her cousin. She had Binney cousins who lived in Detroit and St. Louis whom she had never met, so it wasn't impossible that there were Tipson ones in New England. Still, her father would have known. And he would at least have *mentioned* them to her mother. Wouldn't he?

But Tip had seemed surprised, too. Even though her name was Tipson.

"Oh, murder!" came Gail's whisper from the seat behind.

Corry looked up. Mr. Harmill was collecting the papers at the front of each row.

"On his desk," Gail hissed.

Another stack of papers, held together with a rubber band, lay atop the books lined up between the two rocks Mr. Harmill used as bookends. Corry's heart sank.

It was yesterday's quiz. Already! She closed her eyes, resting her chin on her hands, and behind the cover of her fingers mouthed *Oh please, God, don't let it be an F. Please?*

When she looked up, the quiz papers were coming back the row and Mr. Harmill was watching her with a faint frown. She dropped her eyes to her algebra book and tried to look absorbed. When Jack Loman turned to pass back the corrected quizzes, she took her own and handed the last three on to Gail, trying to keep up the look of earnest concentration as she turned back to her book. Opening out the sheet of paper and folding it flat again in one quick motion, she looked at the letter scrawled in green pencil.

D—.

The relief was wonderful. Corry listened eagerly to Mr. Harmill's comments about Thursday's assignment as he scrawled it across the blackboard, and once she had copied it down in her notebook, she surrounded it with a border of dancing stick figures. Only when she found herself lost midway through the problem Annie Corso was demonstrating at the blackboard did relief give way to gloom. D— was, after all, only a whisker away from F, and the difference wasn't going to be much help when averaged in with her earlier quiz grades and the F from her midterm test. Her homework grades were almost always good, but tests counted more. Her stomach tightened unpleasantly.

Worst of all, five minutes before the end of class, just as Rick Graham was going up front to demonstrate the solution to the problem that had given Corry more trouble than any other in the chapter, the thing she always dreaded most happened. Mr. Harmill called her name.

"Corry? Corry, come up and show us how you would solve this." He erased a patch of blackboard and wrote:

$$2x - 3y = -2$$
$$4x - 12y = 8$$

A snort erupted somewhere in the back of the classroom, but was quickly smothered. Corry tried to pretend she hadn't noticed, but as she moved up the aisle, she felt flushed and miserable. On a second look, however, the equation wasn't such a stinker as Rick's—and it was very like one of those she had gone over twice in the homework assignment. She was able to multiply, add, and substitute her way through to the solution slowly but without stumbling, and—just as Rick finished explaining the procedure he had followed—was saved by the bell. Blessed bell!

"That's it, then," Mr. Harmill said. "Good work, Corry." He spoke loudly enough to be heard over the banging shut of books and general bustle as the classroom emptied. More quietly he added, "Where's your next class, Corry?" as she passed his desk on her way to the door.

"It's art appreciation. Upstairs," Corry said, giving a nervous look at the blackboard. "Did I make a mistake?"

"What? No, no. That *is* good work. That's part of the reason I want to talk to you." Mr. Harmill looked at her kindly and ran a hand through his thinning hair. "Look here, Corry—I can't help seeing that these test and quiz scores really get you down. But you and I both know it's not that you can't do the work. It just *takes* you too long. Now, that's frustrating, but it shouldn't make you look like your last, best friend just died. What is it? Do you get a lot of flak at home about the grades?"

Corry nodded, wordlessly.

Mr. Harmill sighed. "Well, since you're taking college prep courses, they do have to worry about your average. I could suggest a tutor to them."

" 'Her.' There's just my mom. And I don't think we could afford it."

"Um. Then I'd say try doing the assignments through two or even three times." He shrugged helplessly. "You may not have a mind for numbers, but from what my wife tells me, you're a very talented artist. My guess would be that you have a strong figurative imagination, and that's great."

Mrs. Harmill had been Corry's art teacher back in middle school. "Thanks," she said awkwardly.

"Rick Graham, now, he has what I'd call an abstract intelligence, so he does very well at math. They're two different ways of perceiving and reasoning. Take simple arithmetic, for example: If I were to say, 'Rick, Corry, make me a symbolic representation of eight times nine equals seventy-two,' what would *you* do? Show me."

The bell rang as he was picking up a piece of chalk from the chalk tray. He held it out to her. "It's OK. I'll write you a pass."

Corry took the chalk reluctantly, but after erasing the center blackboard she began with quick, free lines to sketch a table, and the ceiling above it hung with party streamers. Circles and squiggles became party guests. A tall, stooped old man and a plump-bosomed, plump-hipped old woman took shape in the foreground. They stood half facing the table, to which in a moment was added a much-candled birthday cake decorated with a large 72. The drawing, full of a wacky comic gaiety, was finished in less than a minute.

"Good heavens!" Mr. Harmill looked from the cartoon to Corry with wonder and suspicion. "I can see by their figures—excuse the pun—that she's the eight and he's the nine, and I suppose they're old because they're the two highest digits, right? But whose birthday is it? And why?"

Corry was embarrassed. "His. Because seven and two make nine."

Mr. Harmill shook his head wonderingly. "It's a classic kind of memory device, but it beats me what it has to do with multiplication. And you didn't make it up just now, did you? You worked too fast for that."

She flushed. "No," she said unhappily, knowing how idiotic it was going to sound. "It's how I taught myself the multiplication tables. Every number has—h-had an age and a sort of personality. Then I would figure out some relationship or scene so I could remember the answer. Look, I *know* it's dumb—"

37

He held up a hand. "If it works, it works. What did—what do you do when you're multiplying double or triple digits? Count the tens on your fingers?"

"Yes," Corry half-whispered.

Mr. Harmill smiled. "Cheer up. It's certainly a handicap, but it's no crime. You look as if you were confessing to running off to Las Vegas with the proceeds of the African Famine Fund collection. To tell the truth, with a technique like that, I'm impressed that you've made it as far as Algebra II. I'll see if there's anything I can work out in the way of some tutoring." He scrawled his name at the bottom of a hall pass. "But for now all I can say is 'Keep slogging along.'"

"Mr. Harmill?" Corry said tentatively.

He looked up.

"What kind of 'symbolic representation' do you think Rick would have drawn?"

Without answering, Mr. Harmill half-turned in his chair and reached out to write on the blackboard

$$8 \times 9 = 72$$

"Oh. *Oh*," Corry said despairingly.

Mr. Harmill gave her an encouraging grin. "Face it. You wouldn't want to be an accountant or an engineer even if you made all As in math. You're an artist. Enjoy it."

Enjoy it. Well, if you counted cake art, maybe some day she could. She had a plan, and if everything worked out. . . . Her mother would hit the ceiling, but if it was all planned out, right down to where the money was to come from, it just might work. She arrived at the art classroom without, oddly, even a twinge of indigestion.

On her way to her last-period class in anatomy and physiology, Tip Meredith appeared from nowhere and fell into step beside her.

"Look," he said awkwardly. "I didn't mean what I said at lunchtime the way it sounded. For all I know, Great Grandfather could have been married to my great-grandmother *and* yours. At different times, I mean. But doesn't it make you wonder—why I never heard about you? Or you about me?"

"Ye-es," Corry admitted.

"So? If it's a mystery, don't you think we ought to solve it?"

Before Corry could answer, he plunged on. "Listen, could you come home with me after school? It isn't far, and there's something I want to show you. Something about your great-grandmother."

"I can't," Corry answered. "If I miss the school bus, I have to walk all the way down the hill home, and the sidewalks are all snowed up. It'd be dark before I got there."

Tip opened the lab door. "That's all right," he said hurriedly. "I'll get you home almost as soon as the bus would. I promise. I'll meet you down by the door outside the cafeteria."

"But I *can't*," Corry objected faintly as Tip strode off to his lab station.

"What was that all about?" Gail whispered excitedly as Corry pulled the *Textbook of Anatomy and Physiology*

39

out from her jumble of papers and textbooks and shelved the rest.

"What was what all about?" Corry evaded. She stared at the box from which Jim George was producing a specimen packet for each lab station. *Cats!* Every dissection project was worse than the last, she thought despairingly. *Why* couldn't there have been a Biology II class this year? The anatomical drawing was fascinating, and Gail was willing to do more than her share of the dissecting, but. . . .

"You know exactly what I mean, Corry Tipson. Tip Meredith. I saw him chasing after you down the hall. Did he ask you out? Did you ask *him?* For Friday night, I mean."

"No." Corry felt a stab of pity for the poor cat as she watched Gail cut open their specimen vacuum pack and pour the preservative into the sink. "And—well, yes, kind of."

"For crumbs' sake, yes *what?*" Gail hissed as soon as Mrs. Burkhardt had given directions for the first steps in preparing the specimens for study.

"Yes, he asked me to go—out with him. I said no." Corry turned on the water in the sink to rinse the formalin off their—specimen. It was easier if you didn't even think the word "cat."

"You didn't. You've got to be *kid*ding." Gail looked at her in despair. "You're *hope*less."

Corry considered. Maybe she was. But people—even cousins—you hadn't known forever were—alarming. You never knew what they were going to say. Or what they really meant when they *had* said it.

Gail, on the other hand, was comfortably predictable.

The only words she spoke for the rest of the class hour were "Where's the other scalpel?" but at the bell, after another sigh of "Hopeless!" she gave Corry's hair a friendly tug just as she had been doing since first grade.

"I forgot to tell you at lunchtime," she said. "Mrs. Dominick said there was a letter or something in her mailbox for you, and you're to ask her for it in case she forgets. I'll see you on the bus."

The "or something" her homeroom teacher produced was a large envelope from the Harlan Hotel Trades Institute in Pittsburgh. Corry had written to them seven long weeks ago. Back out in the hallway, she ripped the envelope open and thumbed through the illustrated brochure to the third page. There, under *Entrance Requirements,* she paused to read *Enrollment is open to students meeting the following requirements: a) graduation from an accredited high school; or b) the equivalent.* Nothing about a minimum grade-average. Further along, under *Training Programs* she found just what she had hoped to find: *Pastry Cook—basic and master courses.*

Stuffing brochure and envelope into her bookbag, she wound her muffler around her coat collar and—perhaps because she felt suddenly cheerful—surprised herself by turning back from the main door and the school buses that could be seen loading at the far side of the parking area. Instead, she hurried down the stairs and out the exit beside the cafeteria.

"Good," was all Tip said when he saw her. He wore earmuffs, and a muffler that matched the thick white wool

41

sweater under his open ski jacket, but no gloves. He looked pleased that she had come, but awkward. His brief spell of talkativeness seemed to have dried up, and he led the way down the graveled walk in silence, hands in his pockets.

At the foot of the hill they crossed the street and headed down Anderson Boulevard. "How far is it?" Corry asked after several minutes.

"Not far. About twenty minutes' walk."

"Oh, great! That's a *mile.*" After a moment, she ventured, "Wouldn't one of the buses get you closer?"

"I like to walk." He slowed. "Don't you?"

"I don't mind."

"A hundred years ago even little kids walked three and four miles to school." Suddenly animated, he turned to grin at Corry. "If they did it now, they might still get there faster than the bus. Besides, it's good for you."

"Try telling yourself that when you miss the school bus and have to walk three miles uphill on a bowl of cornflakes," Corry said drily as she shifted her bookbag to her other shoulder.

"They had it all over us there, too," Tip observed. "They ate *real* breakfasts: porridge and sausage and eggs. Or maybe a stack of pancakes. Even steak."

"Steak. . . ." Corry sighed. "What does steak taste like?"

Tip turned to give her an uncertain look. He had flushed, and Corry wished for a pothole big enough to swallow her up. She didn't even know why she had said it.

"Sorry. Just kidding." She managed a weak grin.

. . .

42

They climbed winding Park Way up from the traffic light by the Riverview Greenhouses in silence. By the time Tip turned off onto Elysian Way, a narrow street with large houses along both the hillcrest up to the left and the slope falling away to the right, Corry was distinctly nervous. If his house and his parents were as rich as his sweater. . . . She heard her mother's familiar, sharp "For Pete's sake, comb your hair back and use one of those little rubber-band things!" and "Are your fingernails clean?" so clearly that she almost looked uneasily over her shoulder.

At the end of a long stretch of tall evergreen hedge, a mailbox with reflector letters spelling out DRESSLER–MEREDITH stood at the foot of a long driveway so neatly cleared of snow that it must have been swept, as well as shoveled or snow-blowered. Maybe, Corry thought, that was what gardeners tended to in wintertime: snow. Would that make them "snowers?" Or "snowmen?"

"What's the 'Dressler' for?"

"That's Great-Grandmother," Tip said. "She married Mr. Dressler after Great-Grandfather died."

"You mean she's still alive? And they live with you?" Corry asked breathlessly as Tip lengthened his stride going up the drive.

"No. Mr. Dressler's dead. And Great-Grandmother's in what I guess you call a 'nursing home.'" He lashed out at a snowy overhead branch. "My parents filed her away under O. For 'Out-of-Sight-Out-of-Mind.'"

From the bottom of the drive, little had been visible above but steep-pitched rooflines and a pointed turret, but soon Corry's heart began to pound with more than the

43

climb. Step by step the house rose out of the snow like a dwelling in a dream—or in a fairy tale. White stucco with dark slate roofs and cut stone framing its tall, arched windows, it even had a plump, round tower that might have come from a fairytale French chateau. Nothing could have looked less like the sober, almost stodgy solidity of the Tipson house on Fourth Street. Surely Lucas Henry Tipson couldn't have built both?

"Is the house hers? Your great-grandmother's, I mean. Or your folks's?"

"Hers," Tip said. "Here, around this way. I—we don't use the front door in winter."

The side door led into a little hallway with a row of curved wooden hooks for coats. As Tip shut the door, Corry unwound her scarf and began to unbutton her coat.

"Don't take your coat off. The heat's turned down low, and we're going up to the attics anyway. It's cold up there." Entering the kitchen, he switched on the large convector heater that stood in one corner.

Corry wanted to ask "Isn't anybody else home?" but Tip was so touchy he might think she meant she was afraid to be alone with him. She wasn't absolutely sure that she *wasn't*—just a little—but after all he was her cousin. And she didn't want to make him go all prickly again. Even so, she kept the heavy bookbag over her shoulder as she followed him through the kitchen and up the narrow stairway opening off the cupboard-lined room beyond.

The attics, a series of raftered rooms and a round, turret-top room, were dimly lit by naked light bulbs and crowded with crates, trunks and furniture, with only a narrow path to the next room left clear. The last room, entered through a narrow, cupboard-style door, was small and less crowded.

"Here—this is part of what I wanted to show you," Tip said. He raised the humped lid of an old brass-bound trunk and, pulling back the folds of what looked like a linen tablecloth, lifted out a rustling waterfall of ivory silk taffeta.

Corry dropped her bookbag with a thump.

It was the gown in the old photograph: puff-sleeved, high-necked and small-waisted, its bodice embroidered in silk and seed pearls with a tracery of roses, vines, and leaves.

"It's hers!" Corry whispered. She reached out a hesitant hand, as if the fabric might disintegrate at her touch. It was crisp and heavy. "It's *beautiful*."

Tip held it up against her coat. "Hold it there," he said. While she did, he opened the quilted silk envelope that had lain beneath the dress and brought out the pearl tiara of the photograph. He fitted it on her head, then bent to drag the trunk and a wooden crate away from in front of the tall old pier-glass mirror against the wall. He used the tablecloth to wipe the dusty glass.

"Wait a minute. Don't look until I tell you." He reached across in front of the mirror and pulled down the faded bedspread that covered the object leaning against the wall beside it.

"There!" he said.

Corry saw her red-gold hair, the pearls, and the ivory gown agleam against attic shadows, and beside her mirrored image a dusty second image in a tall, gold frame: the same red-gold hair glimmering with pearls, the same ivory gown and, on the table where the other girl's hand rested, a Lotus Ware goblet as delicate as a seashell atop a branch of coral.

"*There's* the mystery," Tip said, pointing.

The painted girl's face was scarred, and the canvas torn, as if some sharp object had been thrown against it with great force.

And under the dust of years past, the shards and splinters of the Lotus cup lay strewn across the floor.

Four

"**I** FOUND EDNA'S DUSTPAN," Tip said, reappearing from his foray downstairs. "Is this what you meant by a 'whisk broom?' "

Corry stared at the light-weight longhandled broom and then at her exceedingly strange new cousin. She almost said, "You've got to be kidding," but managed instead to give a shrug. "It'll do. Who's Edna?"

"Mrs. Frowd. I guess you could call her the housekeeper, even though she only works here part time. Mr. Frowd—Jim—is the gardener. But he's only part time, too," Tip added hurriedly, almost as if he were embarrassed that they were there at all.

Maybe he was. As Corry began carefully to sweep together the scattered pieces of the cup, she guessed that he must have decided that her crack about steak meant she actually never *had* eaten one; that she was really poor. A sort of Tipson Cinderella. So now he was going to lean over backwards to try to make all—all *this* seem somehow more ordinary? She felt a twinge of guilt. She supposed she really had been taking a swipe at either his standoffishness or affluence. But it would be horrible if he started being "kind." The Tipsons might always be hard-up, but Corry's mother had once gone off like a rocket at hearing her use the word "poor." "If you think we're 'poor,' miss, you need a new set of eyes and ears. There's folks with roofs that don't keep all the weather off. There's folks eating twenty-five-cent-a-box macaroni and cheese all the last half of every month. You ask over at the Salvation Army, and they'll tell you worse'n that. And then you shut your mouth."

"Here," Tip said when Corry had heaped up a dusty little pile. "I brought this to put the pieces in." He handed her a plastic refrigerator box. It still smelled faintly of chicken livers, and Corry wondered whether he had taken it out of the dishwasher unwashed.

"Thanks." She got down on her hands and knees and, blowing the dust from each piece, placed them carefully in the box. "It doesn't look like there are enough bits to *make* a cup. There must be more."

"I'm afraid some of it's past saving," Tip said hesitantly. "I stepped on one piece when I first uncovered the painting. I heard it crunch."

They found several more pieces and a few splinters, but finally gave up. To recover every chip and sliver they would have to move the tall chest of drawers in the corner, and most of the trunks and boxes. That would take a lot more time than Corry had to spare if she was to get home in time to put dinner in the oven.

"It's four-thirty. I *have* to be home by a quarter past five. How are we going? By taxi? Down Avondale by sled?" Hardly by taxi. She didn't think there was one nearer than Chester, across the river.

Tip turned to lead the way back out through the attics. "I've got a car," he half-mumbled, as if he were admitting to having foot-rot.

Down in the warm kitchen Tip produced two cans of root beer, glasses, and a bakery box of glazed doughnuts.

"What about tomorrow?" he asked as he sat down at the kitchen table across from Corry and took a doughnut from the box between them.

Corry shook her head. "Tomorrow's my mom's day off. I have to be home on the dot and at the homework."

"Maybe I can talk Jim Frowd into giving me a hand with moving that chest and the boxes." Tip hesitated for a moment, and then pushed the box of china fragments across the table and said awkwardly, "You keep them. It was hers, so it ought to be yours."

Corry's eyes shone. "Gosh! Are you sure? If you find all the pieces, and I can stick it back together, it might be really valuable."

"Not to a collector. Only a perfect piece would be really valuable. Unless," he explained earnestly, "it was something a lot older or rarer than Lotus Ware. Even then, perfect pieces are worth five or ten times as much as ones

49

that have been broken and restored—unless they're like the pre-Columbian pottery figures from down near Vera Cruz that my dad collects. The Indians smashed them deliberately as a part of a funeral ritual."

"Vera Cruz in Mexico?" Corry asked. The way he had said it, she could tell that he assumed anyone would know exactly what kind of pottery figures he meant. "Pre-Columbian," she remembered from Mrs. Giorgiadis's comments about the slides of Mexican pyramids she showed in class, only meant "before Columbus."

Tip had that faintly startled, almost apologetic look again. "Yes. Actually, they're pretty neat. They have laughing faces—not like Aztec or Toltec or Mayan art, all grim or dignified." He finished off his root beer. "Maybe we ought to get going."

Corry half wished that Gail could have been on hand to see her arrive at the house on Fourth Street in Tip's yellow VW Golf. It would have sent her into a high dither of pleasure, helpful hints, and heavy campaign plans. Her continual fretting over Corry's boyfriend-less state could be irritating—depressing, even—however well-meant. And even with her advice repeatedly ignored, Gail hadn't lost hope. Thinking about it, Corry tried not to grin as she thanked Tip and slammed the car door.

Gail would hear about it, though. From Don. He was out in front of the Chappicks' house, scraping away with a snow shovel at the hard-packed patches on their sidewalk, and stopped to look and wave. Corry gave an answering wave from the Tipson porch and disappeared into the house,

leaving Don to lean on his shovel in (she hoped) amazement. It would do him good. Take his mind off Angie.

Once she closed the oven door on the tuna-fish casserole her mother had prepared before going off to work, and
had seen to the furnace, Corry went upstairs to ask old Mr.
Hankins about the kerosene.

"That's very thoughtful of you, Cordelia." Mr. Hankins fumbled the chain lock open. "I meant to step across
to the Chappicks' on the weekend to leave enough money
for five gallons, but it slipped my mind." He motioned her
inside and closed the door against the chill of the upstairs
hall. "Then this snow came. I'm afraid I don't like to trust
my old bones to snowy streets and sidewalks. Not many of
our neighbors are as thoughtful as you and your mother
about always keeping a path clear."

He bustled on ahead to open the door from the little
entrance hall into the living room. "Just you keep Mrs.
Hankins company in here where it's warm, and I'll fetch the
money for the kerosene."

Warm? The room was almost as chilly as the hall.
Corry looked around uncertainly. She had always wondered
what the Hankins's nest looked like, but had never before
been past the hall door. It was very dim. She had an impression of walls and table-tops crowded with picture frames
and bric-a-brac, but could not see anything clearly. Several
thicknesses of plastic had been neatly taped over the windows, and the curtains were half drawn.

"Mrs. Hankins?"

"Oh, I'm here, my dear." Mrs. Hankins's high, soft
little laugh tinkled out from a shadowy high-backed arm-

chair. The lamp beside her blinked on. "Do sit down, Corry. George won't be a minute. And it's a long while since we've had a visitor. I'm afraid I don't go out any more. Not even to St. Stephen's. Because of the stairs, you know."

Mrs. Hankins, white-haired, short, and plump, looked a bit like a small, bright-eyed mouse-woman peeping out from a nest of knitted blankets. Her tiny slippered feet rested on a tiny footstool. She had had a bad heart for years.

"How—how have you been feeling?" Corry asked awkwardly. She wasn't sure it was a question she ought to ask, but it was the only one she could think of.

Mrs. Hankins's bright dark eyes smiled at her. "Oh, quite well, now that I've given up the stairs and the kitchen. George takes such care of me, you'd think I was a piece of fine porcelain. Would you believe? He's learning how to cook! He's doing his first roast chicken on Saturday. For our anniversary. Our fifty-sixth."

Corry, whose ears had pricked up at the word "porcelain," found herself staring over the back of Mrs. Hankins's chair at three plates hanging on the wall between the two front windows. "That sounds great," she answered vaguely.

"Ah, you've spied George's plates." The old lady beamed. "They may not be porcelain, but they're as nice as anything in the museum, now aren't they?"

"They sure are—different," Corry said, and then realized how its sounded. "I mean, I like them," she said hastily. "I really do. But they *are* different." She moved across the room for a closer look.

They were shallow, thin, sharp-edged, and perfectly square. Their colors were pale—ivory, peach and raspberry

—and on each three zigzag lines of the other two colors and a pale lime angled across one side. The effect was, oddly, both modern and old-fashioned. Corry was reminded of a color slide Mrs. Giorgiadis had shown one day in class of a design on a painted folding screen. "1930s Modern." Or was it 1920s? Other plates, less odd but still unusual, hung on the other walls among the old family photographs and prints of Niagara Falls and steamboats on the river.

"Where'd they all come from?" Corry asked.

"George made them," Mrs. Hankins whispered proudly as Mr. Hankins reappeared in the hallway and closed the bedroom door.

He crossed to where Corry stood and put a folded envelope in her hand. "Put that in your pocket for young Don, and pass along our thanks."

Hesitantly, Corry asked, "Why didn't you just call him up?" As soon as the question was out, she wished it weren't. What if they hadn't been able to pay their bill and the phone company had cut off their service?

Mr. Hankins nodded. "Ah, well, yes. I'm glad you ask." He smiled gravely, seeming not to notice her embarrassment. "I really should have told your mother last week that we had the line disconnected. Mrs. Hankins has had some medical expenses, and since we must have heat and power, and because I am a firm believer in eating sensibly, the telephone seemed the only place to make a saving. I knew that in any medical emergency your mother wouldn't mind phoning the ambulance service."

"Oh, no. Anytime," Corry said, adding awkwardly, "I mean, sure, but I hope you—she won't have to. Ever." Then, making a lunge toward a safer subject, she said, "I didn't know you were a potter. Did you *really* make these?" She nodded at the plates.

Mr. Hankins smiled. "Yes. Many years ago. At least, my friend Albert McCloskey made the plates and I decorated them. A potter, no. A mere hobbyist. Albert too. He sold cars! I was a shoe salesman for forty-five years. But we both learned a lot from his father, who was a decorator at K. T. and K."

Old Mr. Hankins, who always looked tall because he was so thin, seemed to grow taller still. "Old Mr. McCloskey was very patient with me, and Albert and I did in the end make some fine pieces in that garage of theirs. Even though we sold hardly a one. They were too 'peculiar,' everyone told us. But we kept at it in a small way until shortly before Albert died, seven—no, eight years ago."

"George, show Corry my favorite," Mrs. Hankins said.

Her husband moved to the mantelpiece and reached down an oval plate. Carefully removing the wire-and-spring plate holder, he handed the fragile oval to Corry, who drew in her breath in surprise.

"That," he said, almost shyly, as he crossed the room to sit beside his wife, "is from the set we made as a wedding gift for Mrs. Hankins."

"And we have every piece of it still," Mrs. Hankins announced proudly, giving his hand a squeeze. "I never broke so much as a cup handle."

The plate's face was of a dark, lustrous blue with a sprinkling of silvery pinpoints of stars and a great, shimmering ivory moon just to one side of center. Like the square plates it had a very shallow curve to it rather than the usual raised dinner-plate rim. Unlike most plates, too, its underside was glazed the same faintly irridescent blue as its face. On its base, written in gold, was:

GBH

1930

AMcC

Corry looked up. "It's beautiful," she whispered. "It's so beautiful it—it *hurts*." Very carefully, she put the plate down among the trinkets on a nearby table.

Mrs. Hankins laughed a little silver tinkle of a laugh.

"George promised me the moon and stars—and gave them to me many times over."

Mr. Hankins shook his head and smiled. "Our *real* treasure is there on the mantelpiece. In the center. It's a piece Albert's father decorated back when K. T. and K. made Lotus Ware. Do you know what Lotus Ware is?"

"Yes." Corry peered at the slender-necked little black pitcher with the white rose vine twining up around its body. "Our class went to the museum this week. I think there was one like this there."

"It was our wedding gift from Albert's mother," Mr. Hankins explained, almost reverently.

"I like your plate better. I really do," Corry said.

"Oh, no." Mr. Hankins sounded almost shocked. "The ewer is *Lotus* Ware. Quite rare. K. T. and K. made it for only five or six years. A collector might have to pay seven or eight hundred dollars nowadays for a piece like that." Laying a finger aside his nose, he gave her a mischievous look. "It's generally thought the secret formula died with Joshua Poole, who developed it. But I know better."

"Eight *hundred?*" Corry stared.

Eight hundred dollars! Once Corry had telephoned Don and learned that, yes, he could use his dad's car for a kerosene run, that eight hundred dollars was all she could think about. As she pulled on her coat, then went out, locking the back door after her, she was figuring in her head. If a pitcher in blah black was worth eight hundred, then her great-grandmother's fairytale goblet would have been worth two or three times as much. Maybe as much as two thousand. If it hadn't been smashed. But if it could be mended. . . .

Corry closed the shed door and carried the two empty kerosene cans out the narrow snowy walk between the houses, she was still figuring. If, as Tip said, a perfect piece was worth four or five times a mended one, the cup might still be worth—four or five hundred dollars. Say two or three, since it had been so badly broken. Two or three hundred dollars toward Harlan Institute's pastry-cook courses.

Don loaded the kerosene cans, and one of the Chappicks's own, into the trunk of his father's old blue Chrysler. "I didn't know Meredith had a car," he said. "Is it his? He doesn't drive it to school."

"He's kind of funny. He's got this thing about 'the good old days,' " Corry said, coming back to the real world. "If it was a horse and buggy, now, he'd drive *that* to school."

"I didn't know you knew him," Don said as he slid into the driver's seat. "Except from class."

"I don't. Anyhow, not very well," Corry amended.

Half of her wanted to tell Don the whole story about old Lucas Henry, the two great-grandmothers, and Tip's being her cousin, but the other half rather liked living a private mystery—and stirring up a little curiosity. "He—took me out for a root beer."

"Um. Well, just so he doesn't decide to join Angie's Menagerie." Don grinned. "With his clothes *and* a new car, you might as well just put most of the rest of us out of our misery."

Mrs. Tipson frowned as she scooped ice cream into two dessert dishes.

"I don't like their getting rid of the phone. Not one little bit. What if Mrs. Hankins had a heart attack while the both of us were out? Mr. H. could try the neighbors, but by the time he got to a phone, it could be too late. Every minute counts. That's what they told Mom after Dad had that last attack of his." She sighed. "One thing's for sure. It means I can't raise the rent on them. Not when all they got left to cut down on is food. Drat! Last time I raised it was three years ago, and the way water and everything's gone up, we're long overdue."

"Couldn't we maybe get a long cord and put our phone out on the hall table?" Corry ventured.

Mrs. Tipson was startled out of her frown. "I guess we could. Sure. You know Mr. H. would never take advantage. He—hang on. I got an idea."

She shoved the ice cream box back into the freezer and banged out through the swinging door into the hallway, reappearing almost as soon as she had vanished.

57

"I *thought* that's what it was. There's this old phone-connection box down behind the hall table. It must be where your grand-folks kept the phone before they divided off the upstairs for an apartment. The phone company'll probably have to put in a new jack, but maybe they won't have to rewire. I'll call tomorrow and ask."

When the dishes were done, Corry got out her anatomy book and dissection notes and tried to settle down to making detailed diagrams and drawings from her classroom sketches—work she usually enjoyed. But the *swish-swish* of the flour sifter and clattering whirr of the mixer as her mother set about making the first layers for Mrs. Oakley's cake—sounds she was used to tuning out—kept her from concentrating. Or something did. After she twice mislabeled the same tendon as muscle and vice versa, she concluded that it was Tip's "mystery." On the ride into town he had asked her not to tell about the family connection. *Why?* And why had she promised? Already she was bursting to tell her mother.

Eventually the anatomy report was finished, and Corry moved on to world history. The work went quickly, since she had only a short chapter to read, and at eight-thirty she surfaced to find her mother in her rocker in the far corner of the big old kitchen, dozing in front of the TV while the second batch of layers baked.

There was still the icing globe to finish. Corry retrieved it from the open tea-towel-lined shoebox in the middle of the wide table and examined it for cracks. Not a one! By the time the buzz of the oven timer stirred Mrs.

Tipson from her rocker, the globe was circled with thin icing-ceramic continents cemented on with gum arabic glue, and Corry was using a pastry bag with a No. 4 decorating tube to pipe beading onto their surfaces and along the lines of latticework criss-cross the open "oceans."

"Oh, honey, it's beautiful!" Mrs. Tipson exclaimed, coming for a look after the cake pans were safely upside-down on racks. "It's gonna be perfect! And you know what I got today for on top? Look here."

She went to her handbag and from a plastic packet produced a tiny metal figure which she stood on the table-top. He stood with his legs spread wide and his arms up-stretched in triumph, a sword in one hand.

"I thought we could snip off his sword, paint him white, and stick him on top. 'On Top of the World'."

Corry laughed. "He's from Dungeons and Dragons or one of those, isn't he? He's perfect!"

Finishing the beading, she propped up the world to dry, washed the decorating bag and tube, and dragged her stool over to the equipment cupboard. There, from among the little jars of matte enamel on the top shelf she took the white one, and picked through the brushes standing in a marmalade jar.

Her mother looked up from turning the cakes out of their pans. "While you're up there, see how many Dick-and-Janes we have. I got a wedding coming up week after next, and Mrs. Denney over at church says there are a couple more before June I might get orders for."

Corry looked behind a sack of plaster of Paris and the rubber mold from which the Dick-and-Janes—the stiff

little bridal couples who stood atop Mrs. Tipson's cakes—
were made. For each wedding Corry painted them to match
the coloring and clothing of the real bride and groom.
"There're only two."

"You know," Mrs. Tipson said, tilting her head for a
calculating look up at her daughter, "we could do with our
own special Dick-and-Jane—kind of a trademark?—instead
of using that old store-bought mold."

Corry looked down. "You mean make one? Me? How?
Carve a new model out of plaster?"

Her mother nodded. "And make our own mold. I
think you can buy the rubber stuff at a hobby shop. There's
one over in Columbiana we could write away to."

"No!" Corry said suddenly. She straightened with an
odd, intent look, intent and faraway. What was it Mr.
Hankins had said? She had only been half listening at the
time, but she was sure it was something about most people
thinking the secret Lotus Ware formula was lost—and that
he knew better!

"No? What's 'no' mean?"

Bending to support herself with a hand on the counter,
Corry jumped down.

"It means I've got this really great idea." Her eyes
shone, and she grinned. "But they won't be Dick-and-Janes.
We'll have to call them something snootier. Um . . .
Reginald-and-Elizabeths?"

Five

IF, CORRY THOUGHT as Mr. Cartin wrote the French assignment on the blackboard, there really was a formula. And if it *was* the recipe for Lotus Ware. And, of course, if Mr. Hankins would let her copy it. But if all the ifs came out right, why *couldn't* she make Lotus Ware Reginald-and-Elizabeths? Mrs. Harmill's sixth-grade art class had made pottery Christmas presents—Corry's had been a little decorated wedding cake with *April's Cakes* in raised letters around the bottom tier—and it had been easy. Mrs. Harmill had arranged to have them fired, but afterward there had been no chance to glaze them, so Corry had painted hers and sprayed it with clear plastic, as she did now with the Dick-and-Janes. But glazing couldn't be all that hard—not if you were to use a solid color, like the all-white Lotus Ware. Corry decided she would get a library pass in study hall and look for a book that would explain that part of it.

The Reginald-and-Elizabeth distracted Corry all morning. In English class the discussion might have been going on two rooms away for all she heard of it. A new thought had occurred to her: If all the *ifs* did come out all right, the rediscovery of the process could be more important than any cake-top figurines she might produce. It might even be possible to get credit for the work as an individual study project if she wrote it up afterwards. . . .

At lunchtime Corry was so preoccupied as she went through the cafeteria line that it was only when she was next in line for the cash register that she realized her tray was empty. Red-cheeked with confusion, she stepped out of line and headed back to start over again. The line had grown longer, and when she saw Tike Persons at the rear end, she hesitated. It would be easier to go hungry than to be kidded all the way back down the line.

A hand tapped her shoulder. "Come in here."

Startled, Corry jumped. But it was only Tip, resplendent in a crisp white shirt, black cords, and a diamond-patterned sleeveless black and white sweater.

"I want to talk to you anyway," he said, taking her elbow to draw her into line in front of him.

Corry went rigid with embarrassment, but took the place he offered. No one behind him objected, but that was no comfort. They had all seen her go through the first time and were probably all smothering grins. She didn't look.

"If I had an extra paper bag, you could put it over your head," Tip murmured. "I can't give you mine. I might have an emergency myself."

Corry's Jell-O and whipped cream almost slid off the plate as she set it on her tray and turned. Her eyes widened. "*You?*"

"Cross my heart." He crossed it solemnly, then touched his cheek. "Actually, I keep it on most of the time."

His voice held a wry note, and Corry looked up at him uncertainly. For a moment she thought he might be half serious. But only for a moment. The cashier was waiting, and she had to empty her purse out into her palm to find the right change.

"No—this way," Tip said briskly, catching up to her a moment later. He jerked his head toward a table by the far window.

It meant threading through the tables, and Corry felt sure that every eye was following her. Gail's and Scott's certainly were. They sat three tables away, and from the corner of her eye Corry watched them argue and then change places so that it was Gail, and not Scott, who sat facing the window table. Corry dropped her eyes and kept them firmly on her lunch tray as she unfolded her napkin, opened the milk carton, and then tore a piece off her roll to butter it. She was sure her face was at least as red as the Jell-O.

"What did you want to talk about?" she asked in a low voice.

"I brought you these." He handed her a zip-lock sandwich bag containing several chips from the Lotus cup. Then, taking off his glasses, he searched through his wallet. "And this," he added.

63

"This" was a polaroid photo of the cup itself as it appeared in the painting. "If you do try to restore it, this will give you something to work from. When Mr. Frowd comes on Saturday, I'll get him to help me move the rest of the crates and trunks to be sure we've found all the bits."

The photograph was sharp and clear, and the cup's translucent beauty even more striking than it had been in the shadowed attic. To Corry it seemed almost as if the light shone from within the porcelain itself.

"Hey, it's a really good photograph!" Corry held it up for a closer look, forgetting what she had supposed was a roomful of curious eyes. "You can see even the little knobbles on the 'coral.' "

"I dusted off the whole painting and took this too." He unfolded the wallet's plastic credit card holder and pulled out another photo to pass across to Corry.

It was of the painting itself: Great-Grandmother, ivory gown, ornate little table, Lotus cup and all. The damaged face seemed only blurred, and if Corry had not known it was a painting, she would have thought it simply a color photograph of a young woman dressed in an antique gown.

She frowned. "It's good too, but why carry her in your wallet? That's—*weird*. I mean, she's been dead for umpety years."

Tip shrugged and replaced the photograph in his wallet. "I like it. Besides, the painting's really good. I'd like to find out who painted it, and the next time I go to New York take it to be restored." He leaned forward. "When I dusted it, I found a little brass plaque on the bottom of the frame. Guess what her name is—was."

"How should I know?" Corry took a bite of meat loaf to cover her awe at the unselfconscious way he said, "next time I go to New York." It might have been Gail saying, "the next time I go to the Beaver Valley Mall."

"Take a guess." He bit into his hamburger.

His faintly teasing tone made Corry suspicious. "Was it Cordelia?"

Tip nodded and swallowed. "Yes. Cordelia Ross Tipson. So unless Great-Grandfather had a twin brother, she must have been his first wife. I called the library after I got home again yesterday, and the librarian I talked to said I ought to ask the Secretary of the Historical Society how I might learn more about Great-Grandfather. She gave me his name, and I phoned him after dinner."

"Just like that?" Corry was envious. It had never occurred to her to ask at the library, and talking to strangers on the telephone usually left her tongue-tied or at the very least tongue-twisted.

"Sure." Tip leaned forward eagerly. "He says they haven't any Tipson family papers in their collection—letters, diaries, that kind of thing—but they do have some material from the different Tipson potteries. And I can check on Great-Grandfather's marriages at the Court House in Lisbon. So I'm going over there tomorrow morning."

Corry's spoonful of Jell-O stopped in mid-air. "But tomorrow's only Friday. What about—"

Tip shrugged. "I'll be back before fourth period. I'd

have gone today, but I thought I'd ask whether you'd like to come along."

"Gosh, no. My mom would kill me. Won't your folks mind your cutting classes?"

"I don't think they'd really care. Besides, they're—away," he said, almost evasively. "And Great-Grandmother'll sign an excuse if I ask her."

There really was something odd about her newfound cousin—something she couldn't put a finger on. The more she thought about it, the more convinced she was that his air of competence and cool assurance *was* a paper bag, as he put it. But what was under it?

"Why don't you just ask *her* about Great-Grandfather and the family?" she said.

"I did." Tip frowned. "She went on about how much I looked like him, and how generous he was, and then wandered off into a long, involved story about his investments during World War II in an artificial rubber process. But he died at least fifty years ago, so she had to be mixing him up with her second husband, Mr. Dressler."

"Did you tell her about me?"

"No. This was last week—before I found the painting and knew you had to be closer than a seventeenth or thirty-third cousin. What I did ask was whether Great-Grandfather had any brothers or sisters with families that still lived around here. She said 'No' pretty snappishly, and it was after that her memory began to wander. It made me wonder, and when I found Cordelia and the broken cup up in the far attic, I decided there really was some sort of family mystery. I even thought Cordelia might be a skeleton in one of our closets. But much as I'd like to *know*, I don't want to ask Great-Grandmother any questions that might upset her. Not if I don't have to. That's why I need to go to Lisbon. And the Court House offices aren't open on Saturdays."

He smiled, and Corry—for the first time meeting his eyes directly—saw that he was really very good-looking when he came out from behind the cool, bored look. A little like old Lucas Henry. But only a little.

"Have you started on the cup?" he asked.

"No." Corry finished her milk and looked at her watch as she crumpled her napkin. She wanted to tell about Mr. Hankins's plates and the Lotus Ware formula and her ideas for the Reginald-and-Elizabeth, but that would mean explaining everything, beginning with her mother's wedding cakes, and there wasn't time. Not if she was to stop by the counselors' offices to ask about individual study projects for credit. Besides, he would probably think wedding-cake figurines a pretty Mickey-Mouse project for china as fine as Lotus Ware. The suspicion that he might be right if he did made Corry hold her tongue. She retrieved her bookbag from the floor and pushed back her chair. "I've *gotta* go."

"Why? It's ten minutes till the bell. And I haven't— there was something I wanted to ask you," Tip said, hurriedly putting his glasses back on. He sounded almost anxious. "I'll go with you."

"No. I've got to go up to the office," Corry said firmly. "And you've still got your other whole hamburger and your yogurt to finish."

"No, listen." He snatched at her hand. "I've found the table the Lotus cup is standing on in the painting, and I wondered . . . I thought if I could take a photo of you in Cordelia's gown, in the same pose and lighting, it would—it would be a real help to a picture restorer."

"But only the face was messed up," Corry objected. She freed her hand. "Couldn't we just give him one of my class pictures to go by? Or get a copy made of the old wedding photo?" But the idea of wearing that beautiful gown, of dressing up as her great-grandmother, was tempting. If it didn't sound like little kids' make-believe, she would have thought it might almost be like stepping into the past. . . . But that was silly.

"Oh. I hadn't thought of that." Tip looked startled, then disappointed, but as Corry shouldered her bookbag and stood, the cool detachment returned. Just as if he *had* put on a paper bag.

"If you'll get a print made for my mom, I'll do it," she said suddenly, and was surprised by her own firmness. "But then I'll have to explain about the painting. And your family. I really don't like *not* telling her."

"I'll think about it," Tip said slowly. "I don't know."

Gail, lying in wait outside the cafeteria door, was in a dither of excitement. "What was all that about? You looked so serious, and he—well, he may be stuck-up, but who cares! He's gorgeous. At least, when he takes his glasses off, he is." Corry tried to laugh, and said airily that they had been talking about pottery and painting. It was true enough.

Gail was skeptical. "Oh, sure! But he did ask you out. I could tell. Tomorrow night? Where's he taking you?" They reached the door to the main office before Corry's repeated denials convinced her that Tip had not asked her out. Not even for a Whopper and a movie, let alone dinner at some expensive French restaurant in Pittsburgh and the symphony after. But Gail could not be convinced there was no romance afoot. "The way he was looking at you? Hah!"

As if all that were not bad enough, Mrs. Eckert in the counselors' office explained that applying for approval of an individual study project was not just a matter of finding a teacher to act as adviser, and plunging in. First, Corry would have to write an outline of the project and a description of its educational purpose and value. Then, once the application had both her mother's and Mrs. Giorgiadis's approval, it still had to go through the County Board of Education. Even if Corry turned in an application tomorrow and by some miracle it was approved next week, the project could not be scheduled before the fall semester. Almost six months to wait!

Unless she *didn't* wait, Corry thought afterwards. Why should she? Why not learn on the Reginald-and-Elizabeths, and do something more—well, *serious* for the project? She had given Mrs. Eckert only a vague description of her idea because—sickening thought!—what if after all there was no secret formula? Corry hadn't even had a chance to ask Mr. Hankins whether he really did know where or what it was. *Why*, she fretted, did she always set herself up for disappointment?

Corry usually walked home from the corner of Jackson Street with Don, but today she was out and away as soon as the school bus door opened. The sky had cleared, the last of the snow was melted, and she ran with the yellow muffler streaming out from her hand like a banner in the sudden sunshine.

Up the porch steps, shrugging out of her coat, banging the door shut behind her, slinging the coat and her bookbag onto the hall table, Corry took the stairs two at a time in her eagerness to ask Mr. Hankins the fateful question. In front of the Hankins's door, she stopped to catch her breath, and then gave a quiet knock.

She waited what seemed an endless time. More than once she raised her hand to knock again, but didn't. If Mr. Hankins was out, Mrs. Hankins couldn't help taking an age coming to the door. And it would be awful if she hurried because she thought you were getting impatient. Corry fidgeted for two or three minutes more and finally knocked again, more firmly.

Mr. Hankins opened the door a moment later, and called over his shoulder, "You were right, Doris. There was a knock. Young Cordelia."

To Corry he said with a little bow of old-fashioned courtesy, "Good afternoon, Cordelia. Have we kept you waiting on the doorstep? I'm afraid we were watching television, and didn't hear."

"It wasn't long," Corry said awkwardly, almost in the same breath demanding, "Was it true? What you said? About the Lotus recipe not really being lost?"

"Why, yes." Mr. Hankins seemed taken aback by her urgency. "Won't you come in?"

In the living room, Mrs. Hankins clicked off the game show she had been watching. "Do sit down, Corry. You'll have a cup of tea, won't you? The pot's still hot." She indicated the tray on the coffee table.

Corry shook her head. "I can't stay. I just came to ask—"

"Whether I know Joshua Poole's secret formula for Lotus Ware," Mr. Hankins finished for her. "Now why would you be curious about that?"

Corry took a deep breath. "I have to make some figurines—for Mom's cakes—and the Lotus things are so beautiful I thought it would be wonderful to make them that elegant. Like the cakes. Then once I got good at it," she added shyly, "maybe I could do something special for an independent study project at school next year."

Old Mrs. Hankins gave her a shrewd, curious look. "Like what, Corry?"

"Maybe like this?"

From a pocket she produced Tip's photograph of the painted Lotus cup, and watched anxiously for Mr. Hankins's reaction as he took off his spectacles and held it up for a close look.

"Mercy me!" he said faintly. "Wherever did you see a piece like this? Or is—why, it's a painting, isn't it?"

Corry nodded. "It's from a painting of my great-grandmother. The real cup got smashed to bits."

Mr. Hankins stood frowning at the snapshot, with one hand gripping the back of his armchair, and Corry suddenly realized that he must be standing only because she was. "A real gentleman with real lovely manners," her mother always said. As he moved to show the picture of the cup to his wife, she backed toward the nearest chair and sat down.

Mr. Hankins opened one of the glass-fronted book-cases flanking the fireplace, took out a small book, and returned to settle into the sagging comfort of his armchair. "I do have the 'recipe.' At least, this is one of Joshua Poole's pocket notebooks, with a note of what I believe to be the Lotus formula. But to *use* it . . . I don't know. Albert McCloskey and I often talked of trying it, but it promised to be a great deal of work. A very great deal. I never seemed to have the time, and after I retired, the hours seemed to fly even faster. Then Albert fell ill and passed away. And now here you are, proposing to copy what looks like a masterpiece. Just like that! Have you worked in clay before?"

"Once. In middle school. And we didn't do the firing part," Corry admitted. Her cheeks reddened. "But it can't be all that hard, can it? It must be at least a little bit like baking a cake. Isn't it?"

"It is—a bit," he said doubtfully. "If you have a proper recipe. But this only gives quantities, not directions."

"Tell Corry how you happen to have it," Mrs. Hankins prompted. "Such a piece of luck!"

Mr. Hankins smiled. "When I was a young man, Joshua Poole's son, Joshua Jr., was a customer of mine at the shoe store, and for a short time I rented a room in his house. He remarked one day that he meant to clear his father's papers out of the attic—just throw them away! I jumped at his offer to let me have a look at them and take my pick. I came away with this. Here. You're welcome to have a look at it, Cordelia." He opened the notebook and held it out across the coffee table. "That page."

The leather-covered notebook, worn with use, was dated 1901 and filled with lists of ingredients for china stains, clay bodies and glazes, with unfamiliar ingredients like *spar* and *borasc* and *fritt*. The page Mr. Hankins indicated—loose, slightly larger than the rest, and dated faintly in pencil *1891*—appeared to have been torn from an earlier, perhaps discarded notebook. The four formulas, for a bone china clay body, a china stain to lighten the clay, a "fritt" mixture, and the bone china's glaze covered both sides of the page. In many places the penciled writing was almost rubbed away, and had been lightly overwritten in ink.

Corry frowned. "It doesn't say 'Lotus Ware' anywhere."

"No," agreed Mr. Hankins. "But the date is right. Lotus was made between '91 and '97, and this seems to be the only set of formulae he kept from that period. I've shown it to my young friend Ralph Ginger, who's a ceramic engineer. He doesn't know what else it would *be*."

"I didn't know you had to *make* the clay—the clay 'body.' " Corry hesitated, her forefinger hovering down the lines of numbers and ingredients. "But I could try it," she said softly, looking up. "At least *try*."

Mr. Hankins gave a little sigh. "I wish Albert and I had tried. No question it's worth doing. Yes. Yes, you may copy it. And I shall be happy to help in any way I can."

"Well, *you* look pleased with yourself," Mrs. Tipson observed as Corry swept into the kitchen and gave her an enthusiastic hug. "How's come? Good news on that algebra test?"

Six

"**G**OSH, YOU LOOK like you had slugs and snails and beetle juice for breakfast," Gail observed as she plumped down on the school bus seat beside Corry.

Corry, sitting with her forehead against the cool glass of the window, wrinkled her nose half-heartedly. "I feel like it, too."

"Your old grumbletum again?" Gail asked. Absent-mindedly, she offered Corry a stick of gum before taking one herself. "Oh, sorry. Is it?"

Corry nodded and closed her eyes again.

"How's come? Something happen?"

Corry made a face. "The algebra quiz. Mom asked about it, and when I told her I got another D, she flipped out. You should've heard her."

"No thanks!" Gail had once seen Mrs. Tipson in a fury over a fine for two overdue library books. It had cured her as thoroughly of forgetting library books as it had Corry. "At least it wasn't an F."

"It might as well have been." Corry clutched her book-bag against her chest and poured out in a despairing whisper. "She doesn't even care about As or Fs or whatever any more. It's all grade average. 'What's it now, Corry? Two-point-four-five? That's not good enough, Corry. Two-point-five. It's gotta be at least two-point-five, Corry. What the H am I working my buns off for if you're not gonna get into KSU and make something of yourself? Why'm I standing on my feet eight hours a day? Answer me that!'" KSU was the local campus of Kent State.

Gail looked at her helplessly. "She still wants you to do business math and that computer stuff in college? Why don't you just tell her you *can't*?"

Corry fished a tissue from her pocket and blew her nose, looking around self-consciously. How awful if everyone had been listening! But from the noisy, cheerful conversations on all sides it seemed no one had. And she did feel better for talking about it.

"I sort of—can't."

"What does that mean?"

Corry looked at Gail out from under her fringe of curls, sheepishly. "I sort of painted myself into a corner. I didn't *lie*, but last year when she wanted me to sign up for Business Office Ed., and I knew I'd hate it, I told her I could get a lots better job if I took all that stuff in college instead. And it's true. She went up to school and asked, and Mrs. Eckert told her the same thing. And because I wanted to find out if I *could* do it, I let her think you had to be in

75

the college prep program to get into any college at all." She sighed. "You're lucky. You and Don. Your folks are glad you want to be a teacher. And even if Don's dad's teased him and called him Doctor Doolittle ever since he decided in seventh grade he wanted to be a vet, you can tell he really thinks it's great. Even if he *does* moan about where'll they ever scrape up the money."

"But you've got to tell your mom," Gail said in exasperation. "If she doesn't know what you want to do——"

"Oh, she knows." Corry looked out of the window as the bus came to yet another stop and two more students boarded. A lilac bush in the front yard of the shabby frame house opposite had put out its first small leaves, tiny green flags in the wind that stirred the hillside.

April Tipson knew. Corry, tearful, still cautious, but trying to defend herself, had said, "Why can't I just do what you do? Get any old job, I mean, and bake cakes, too. It's what I like best."

And her mother's red-cheeked anger had given way to angry tears. *Why?* she had raged. Because then there would be no way out. How many hundred-dollar three-tier wedding-cake weddings did Corry think people here could afford? This was a seven-fifty birthday cake and sixty-dollar wedding cake town. No way out. No way back to Pittsburgh, which Corry's grand-parents had so rashly abandoned when April was fifteen. No way back to Pittsburgh where, however bad things were, there was always something going *on*. Hockey games. Clubs with live country music. Or rock. The Syria Mosque, with cheap tickets to hear Johnny Mathis. Or maybe Wayne Newton. She couldn't make it back, couldn't get out of here on her own. Not when she couldn't type. Couldn't even spell. Couldn't couldn't couldn't *read* worth a nickel. Not well enough even for a lot of the recipes in *The Art of Pastry.* And not with a house she couldn't sell even if she didn't have the Hankinses to worry about. Who was going to buy a patched roof and banging pipes and antique wiring and a sagging front porch when there were five hundred and ninety-nine other houses in town for sale? Well, if she couldn't get out from under on her own, she sure as little apples could see that Corry did. Corry could maybe work in one of those tall buildings, all glass, they saw on the TV news out of Pittsburgh. Then they could afford to rent the other half of the duplex house on Beeman Street from Corry's Aunt June and Uncle Russ if it came vacant. And-and-and—Oh why did Corry's dad have to step off the Washington Street curb in the middle of the block away from the streetlight and get himself killed by a driver drunker than he was?

Corry felt as if she had opened Pandora's Box. As if the kitchen were full of wasps. She couldn't handle it. All that she could do was try to shut the box—fast—and pretend all the questions had buzzed safely away out of hearing. "I'll get the cake layers out," she offered anxiously. "And make the sugar glaze, if you want me to." Her face had felt stiff, her smile iced on.

As the bus turned up the high school driveway, she said to Gail, "When everything's all set, I'll tell her. And it'll be all right. I'll go learn fancy baking at Harlan, and then we can rent the other half of Aunt June's house, and open up an April's Cakes shop on—on Fifth Avenue."

77

Gail was startled. "Just like that? You mean you'd leave here for good?"

Unseeing, Corry looked out the window across the folded hills where the maples and poplars showed their first whisper of green, and shrugged. "It's a seven-fifty birthday cake and sixty-dollar wedding cake town. It won't be able to afford us."

Tip had said he was going to Lisbon instead of school, and apparently he had. Corry found herself relieved not to have to worry about his popping up at her elbow when least expected. It wasn't that she wasn't pleased to see him and flattered by the attention, but he always had an air of having time to waste and seemed to expect her to throw hers away too. When she didn't have any to throw away.

Corry's indigestion faded as the morning unrolled from world history though French and English without her being called on. She had to work hard at concentrating—at resisting the temptation to doodle new ideas for the tilt of Reggie's head or the curve of the arm in which Liz would hold her spray of roses. Reaching her third-period classroom a minute or two before the bell, she used the time to start a list under the heading *DO*:

> Ask Mrs. G. about individ. study proj.
> Library—pottery books?
> Copy Lotus recipes
> *Workroom*—where?
> Buy clay where?

Where to work was the biggest problem. The kitchen, well-lit, tile-floored, and with water and the back door right at hand, would be ideal. But fat chance. Her mother would never stand for the mess. The front room in the cellar would be coolest come summer, but even if the walls and ceiling were hosed down and whitewashed and you didn't have to worry about coal dust, it wouldn't do. Every time someone walked across the floor overhead, plain old old-house dust sifted down from between the boards. That left the attic. Which was a mess.

Lunch was a gulped-down chili dog and french fries, and a race up to the library. There, among the entries in the card file under *Ceramics*, Corry found *Practical Pottery and Ceramics*, *The Home Potter*, *The Craft of Ceramics*, and *The Complete Book of Pottery Making*. After skimming through all four, she settled for the last. It seemed to explain processes more thoroughly, and had a solid, serious textbook look to it where the others seemed intended for hobbyists. She checked it out, and stayed to read until the bell rang.

Tip caught up with her after algebra, on the way to Mrs. Giorgiadis's art appreciation class.

"Hey, slow down. I've been looking for you. I just got back." He didn't look as if he had hurried much.

"You find out anything?" Corry asked shyly.

Tip nodded. "A little. We were right. Your Cordelia *was* Great-Grandfather's first wife. They were married in 1900, and she died in 1924. He married my great-grandmother in 1925, when she was twenty-eight, and since by then your grandfather was already twenty-three years old, the split between him and his father can hardly have been because she was a wicked stepmother."

Corry stopped outside the art room door to look at him suspiciously. "Then why are you looking so cheerful?"

"Because I may have found an answer. Great-Grandfather sold Tipson and Perry back to the Perrys in 1927, and he unloaded Tipson and Son—the one that became the Pelican Pottery—to your grandfather for thirty thousand dollars, and Comet China to a—" He checked his notebook. "To a Charles Deagle for fifty thousand dollars in September of 1929. *One month* before the stock market crashed and businessmen started jumping out of skyscraper windows."

He grinned. "Nothing like that here. No tall buildings. I read somewhere that a local character once actually walked away from a three-story fall, so everybody would figure even a step out of the top floor of the Little Building might be survivable. Messy, but survivable."

Corry paled. "Don't joke about it. That's gross!"

Tip looked suddenly awkward. "I'm sorry. I was just—"

But Corry had vanished into the classroom.

Corry spent the minutes before the class bell on a quick new sketch of the Reggie-and-Liz and kept her head resolutely turned away from the table at the back of the room where Tip sat. In the new design the elaborate filigree decorating the skirt of Liz's gown was gone, and the skirt itself had a simple, almost severe elegance. The only elaborate "Lotus" touches would be the spray of roses and filigree on the pedestal.

After class, Corry lingered over her notebook, took her time gathering up her books, and while Bob Wainer talked to Mrs. Giorgiadis about his report on early modern architecture, pretended to read one of the articles pinned on the bulletin board. She was really rehearsing to herself just what she was going to say.

"Did you want to talk to me, Corry?"

Startled, Corry turned to see that Bob was gone, and students from the next class were coming in. They drifted to their seats, laughing and talking.

"I'm afraid it will have to be quick," Mrs. Giorgiadis said.

After all the times she had gone over in her head just what to say, and what would be the best way to say it so that Mrs. Giorgiadis would be impressed both by the Lotus project and by Corry's own determination to carry it through, every one of the graceful sentences deserted her.

"I was wondering . . . I—Do you think you could be my adviser for an independent study project?" she blurted out.

"That would depend." Mrs. Giorgiadis looked both curious and cautious. "What sort of project?"

Corry was distracted by the bustle around her. She found herself as nervous of talking about the Lotus formula in front of strangers as she was about making the project sound interesting enough. It wasn't as if anyone could steal the idea and make a better job of it than she could. But— but if everyone heard about it, if everyone was watching and waiting, it would make it worlds more dreadful if it didn't work.

Mrs. Giorgiadis listened patiently as the half-whispered explanation, awkwardly begun, seemed—at least to Corry—to come out upside-down and backwards. She looked puzzled at first, then surprised, but by the time Corry trailed off she had a look that was, oddly, both faraway and excited. When Corry shyly produced her drawings of Reginald and Elizabeth on their pedestal, she looked up from the sheets of tablet paper in astonishment.

"Why, they're wonderful, Corry! Not at all sticky-sentimental. When you said, 'wedding-cake figures,' I thought, 'Oh, well, for a first few test pieces it won't matter.' Every cake-top pair I've ever seen has looked as stiff and empty-headed as if whoever modeled for them had been stuffed by a taxidermist. But these two—" She touched the penciled figures lightly and shook her head. "You can tell that these two care very much about each other."

"Will you do it, then?" Corry asked anxiously. "Be my adviser, I mean, if I put in an application?"

Mrs. Giorgiadis's smile faded. "I would love to, Corry, but I've never taught ceramics. I did some potting four years ago, in college, but I haven't taught Art IV yet. It has the only ceramics unit we do. I'll be teaching it next year, but the ceramics part doesn't come until after Christmas. I haven't started boning up on it yet. You'll be better off going to—"

Corry was alarmed. "No, it has to be you. I mean, I don't know. . . ."

How could she explain? She did not know either of the other art teachers, and it had been difficult enough ask-

82

ing Mrs. Giorgiadis, whom she knew and liked. How could she ask a stranger?

Mrs. Giorgiadis smiled broadly as she handed back the sketches. "In that case, I wouldn't miss it for anything."

Corry was almost late to her sixth period class, and after class almost missed the bus. Mrs. Giorgiadis had asked her to stop by the art room on her way out, and had presented her with a fat, plastic-wrapped ball of clay.

"For the model you'll make your mold from," she explained. "Why wait until September?"

Why wait indeed? But as Corry raced down the hall and past the library, she saw Tip waiting by the lockers outside her homeroom. It flashed through her mind that she could pretend she hadn't seen him and turn back to the stairs without her jacket and the rest of her books. . . . But in spite of the sunshine, it was too cold a day to go jacketless home. And after last night's explosion, she didn't want to set her mother off again by turning up minus half the weekend's homework.

She hurried to her locker and, with a nod for Tip, fumbled with the lock. "Oh, *nuts*! I'm gonna miss the bus," she moaned as it stuck.

"Corry? I wanted to ask if you'd like to come over tomorrow," Tip said as she tugged the door open and began stuffing books into her bookbag. "You didn't give me a chance to ask before. We could take that photo, have some lunch, and then drive over to Lisbon and around. I saw some antique shops over there. The one I went into had a Pelican bowl, so I bought it. It would be fun to look for more Tipson and Pelican and Comet pieces. Maybe even Lotus."

Corry hesitated for a moment, but then hurried toward the stairs with Tip close behind.

"I told you," she said. "Only if I can tell my mom who you are. I mean, why not? For somebody all fired up about finding out what split the family up back in the Year Zot, you don't seem very interested in *un*-splitting it."

Being shy had never stopped Corry from being stubborn. As much as she was attracted to the idea of trying on Cordelia's gown or of looking for pieces of Pelican China, her resistance to Tip's persuasions had grown along with the suspicion that—"paper bag" jokes or no—his lordly air was all too genuine. OK. If he was too snobbish to want to know a Mrs. Tipson who was a supermarket checker, she could do without Mr. and Mrs. Meredith of Elysian Way.

"Please," Tip said. He followed her outside, striding beside her as she hurried toward the No. 20 bus. "Just the china-hunting, then. Or come and see the bowl."

Corry couldn't tell whether it was a demand or a plea. "Maybe some other time," she said. "I'm busy all weekend."

She had kept an anxious eye on the bus, and suddenly broke into an awkward run, hampered by the heavy book-bag with its extra weight of clay.

Tip strode after her. "Busy with whom?" he wanted to know. Even when he sounded—hurt? ticked off?—he was grammatical.

Corry answered over her shoulder as she climbed aboard the bus. "Reggie and Liz," she called out.

He was still standing there in the parking lot looking baffled as the buses rolled downhill and away.

It was Gail's considered opinion that Corry had gone utterly and tragically off her rocker.

"You're crazy, you know that? Stark, staring, bibble-babble crazy. I saw it through this very window. You did everything but hit him with a rolled-up paper and order 'Down, boy!' What is it with you? Have you been eating toadstools? Sniffing tabasco sauce?"

Corry giggled, but it only made her angrier with Tip and her promise not to tell anyone about the family relationship. It was bad enough to have to avoid the subject with her mother. With Gail it was worse because even without telling an outright lie, she was letting her believe one.

But when she arrived home to find an envelope on the hall table addressed to her in Mr. Hankins's large, spiky handwriting, she forgot about Tip.

Here, the note inside said, was the formula. He had copied it out for her because it might be best if she didn't come upstairs. Mrs. Hankins was not feeling well, and needed to rest. Perhaps tomorrow. As for the ingredients listed, Corry should be able to get quite a few of them down at Mason Color and Chemical Company on Second Street. She could ask at the Potters Supply about a sagger in which to make the frit, the glass which would add to the translucency of both clay and glaze. About the clays he knew nothing. That had been Albert's side of their work.

Corry felt a guilty relief. She was sorry about Mrs.

Hankins, but had half dreaded facing Mr. Hankins again. She suspected he wouldn't have been so willing to give her the formulas if she hadn't let him think she might copy the Lotus cup. As if she could make anything like that!

In the kitchen Corry poured herself a grape soda from the big bottle in the refrigerator and wondered what she ought to do first. There was still time to go down to Mason Color and Chemical before five o'clock, but what would she say to them? That she needed a cupful of powdered lead and a tablespoon of regular china stain for "an old formula?" They'd say "Sorry, we only sell in quantity." But if she tried to get them interested by mentioning Lotus Ware, half the town could end up looking over her shoulder. Besides, there was the money. How much would—she looked at the sheet of paper—five or six pounds of feldspar cost? She had seventeen dollars in the savings account Granny Binney had opened for her three birthdays ago, but that wouldn't last long. She would have to find a summer job. Period.

It was the clay in its plastic bag that decided her. She itched to be at it. And since her mother had *asked* her to do the figurines and hadn't yet declared the kitchen table off-limits. . . . Slipping the papers back into their envelope, Corry went to her bedroom and retrieved the Harlan Hotel Trades Institute envelope from between her mattress and box springs. Tucking Mr. Hankins's envelope inside the larger one, she returned it to its hiding place and hurriedly smoothed down the bedspread.

To protect the kitchen table, Corry brought down from the attic the old oilcloth tablecloth that had covered it in her Grandmother Tipson's day. Doubling it over so that the clay could not muck up the table through the threadbare patches, she spread out her sketches. From the high cupboard shelf she brought down the open sack of plaster of Paris and the old bowl and spoon and measuring cup she used for mixing plaster for the Dick-and-Janes. Beside them she set out two large aluminum pie pans, an old wire cheese cutter that had lain unused at the bottom of the utensils drawer for years, a small, stained wooden lazy Susan that had once held little pots of mustard, ketchup and horseradish but would make a decorating turntable almost as good as her mother's, and a handful of makeshift modeling tools: turkey skewers, a plastic knife, nail file, and an old spool of wire stiff enough to bend into loops for shaving away at the clay.

She made two "bats"—the plaster circles that would be her working surfaces—first, mixing two parts of water into three of plaster, taking care not to mix it too long for fear of stirring in bubbles. Poured out into the pie pans, it hardened in moments into solid cakes. She put them to dry in the oven.

Corry remembered some of the steps that followed from Mrs. Harmill's class back in middle school. The rest she had picked up from her reading. The clay had to be wedged to get rid of air bubbles, which could crack a piece in the pottery kiln, where temperatures might go as high or higher than 1800° Fahrenheit. To wedge her lump, Corry sliced it in half with the old cheese cutter, slammed one half down on the oilcloth-covered table and then the other down on top of it. She repeated the process of cutting and wedging ten times for good measure. The noise and pleasure of being able really to *slam* something without feeling guilty or self-conscious lifted her spirits, and when at last she cut off a lump of the silken clay and placed it on the oven-warm bat she had "sized" with liquid soap so clay would not stick, she was surprised at her own excitement. For a long moment she sat motionless, and then began to pinch and shape and smooth.

When April Tipson came home from work, tired from a long day on her feet and the long walk across town, and ready for dinner, there was none. Corry had forgotten her mother, the spaghetti sauce thawing in the refrigerator, almost her own name. As she smoothed a silken fold with a twisted-wire tool, nothing else in the world existed: only the curve of the silk in her mind's eye, and the echo of it growing beneath her clay-stained fingers.

"For Pete's sake, Corry!" Her mother groaned. "I'm starved, and you haven't even put the sauce out to finish thawing. What the H are you doing?"

Corry gave no sign of hearing—either the question or the angry click of her mother's approaching heels.

Mrs. Tipson stopped suddenly, and then quietly moved closer as she caught sight of the two small figures standing side by side on the plaster bat. Straight and slender, poised in a tension between repose and eagerness, they were turned a little toward each other, leaning a little against the other, looking at each other. Holding hands.

"Oh, honey!" April whispered. "Oh, *Corry.*"

Seven

ORRY WAS UP at six-thirty and startled her mother by appearing in the kitchen in jeans and a T-shirt five minutes later. Mrs. Tipson, who had been enjoying her "quiet hour" before breakfast with a cup of coffee and country music on the radio, looked up in mock alarm.

"You forget it's Saturday, hon, or are you sick?"

"I just couldn't wait," Corry said, lifting the empty milk carton that had covered the Reggie-and-Liz for the night. "Now it's drier, I can work on their faces, and the little details."

She touched the edge of Liz's skirt with her fingernail. The clay had hardened, but not too much. Perhaps not enough.

"Here, now," Mrs. Tipson said as Corry picked up one of the modeling tools. "Don't you start up in here again. You get yourself some breakfast, and then after nine-thirty when Mr. Oakley comes to pick up the cake, you go clear out your studio so's you can move it all up there."

"My what?" Corry, who had been admiring the handsome whipped-chocolate and white-icing fantasy rising out of a cut-down grocery carton, turned to stare.

"You heard." Her mother got up and went to the stove to pour herself another cup of coffee. "You can use the front attic room if you can find somewheres to put all the stuff. You oughta be able to dig out a table and chair good enough to use. Just don't throw anything out we can fix up."

Over the years the worn-out armchair, the torn lampshades, a broken ironing board, a cracked plastic dishpan, and saucers without cups, as well as anything that could be fixed up or made over "if there was just time," had been abandoned at the head of the attic stairs. The large, once-pleasant room might have been a junk-dealer's overflow storeroom.

It was familiar ground to Corry from childhood expeditions and her searches for interesting bits of clothing or fabric for the odd outfits she hid behind at school. She knew that the tiny bathroom and three small rooms beyond the barricade of dusty discards were much less crowded. They would just have to take the overflow. She began by pulling out and piling to one side or the other cartons of old clothing and—strange things to keep!—empty ketchup bottles. When she reached a three-legged bedside table, lifting it up and setting it down behind her, only a chest of drawers stood in her way. A good, hard shove shifted it, and she opened the door beyond.

By noon, the walls in the smaller rooms were lined

with cartons and old furniture. Junk that was repairable, or worth taking to the Salvation Army, was stacked atop them. The narrow iron bedstead in one room was heaped with sacks and cartons of old clothing, some made of fine fabrics and, Corry was sure, more than fifty years old. The bathroom was clean, even if nothing worked but the toilet. The water to the sink and old iron bathtub had been turned off years ago because of leaky pipes.

And the front room had begun to look halfway like a studio. Corry had pushed the two old steamer trunks which stood in the front window gables across to the far wall and placed a table in each gable alcove. One table actually was blessed with four legs of the same length. She mended the short leg of the other by gluing an old red checker to its foot. A chest of drawers—for supplies—stood beyond the stairwell, its missing handles replaced by ones of thin clothesline rope. A large crock and two smaller ones were stowed in two old fruit crates in the corner. They might prove useful. But the ketchup bottles, lampshade frames, and a bag of motheaten clothing and mouse-chewed bedding she carried down to the back yard and dumped by the garbage cans.

The real find was an an antique set of thirty pigeon-holes, perfect for jars and packets of ingredients, and other supplies. They were well-made—from an old office or shop, Corry guessed—and very heavy. She had measured the distance between the two hanging-hooks, driven the nails in the wall, and then found the box of pigeonholes too heavy to lift more than waist-high. They would have to wait until Don could lend a hand.

Once the furniture and floor were damp-dusted, the old oilcloth cut and tacked to the tables, and the fourth leg of the one straight chair glued and nailed in place, Corry dragged up a trunk to serve as a makeshift seat and settled down to sharpening the detail on Reggie and Liz. That done, she used the cheese cutter to pare off the arm that was to hold Liz's flowers. With a plaster mold there could be no undercut areas, or the mold would not separate from the model. The arm would have to be cast separately. For now, all that was left to do was to hollow out the figures so that the clay was of much the same thickness throughout and would not crack in the drying.

Only when the work was finished and the Reggie-and-Liz was left to dry did Corry, suddenly ravenously hungry, remember lunch. After she polished off the cold leftover spaghetti, she found she still had an hour and a quarter before she was to meet Gail at the library. They were going up to the Beaver Valley Mall with Sue Letterman to pick out a joint birthday present for Annie Corso.

But back upstairs, instead of sitting down to reread the chapters on molds and slip-casting in *The Complete Book of Pottery Making*, Corry was drawn to the old chest with the faded tag that said *John's Things*. John. That would be her grandfather. Her grandfather the failure, who owned Pelican Pottery and saw it go bust. If Tip was right, though, maybe that hadn't been his fault. If Great-Grand-father had sold—not given—the pottery to him, he must have had to borrow money to pay for it. Then when the stock market crashed (Corry wasn't really sure what that meant, but Tip had made it sound pretty dreadful), Grandpa probably couldn't help crashing with it. And if he blamed his father. . . .

Corry thought that she had long ago opened everything openable in the attic, but none of the half-empty trunk's contents looked familiar. She took them out one by one: the carefully folded little boy's sailor suit, the young man's tuxedo jacket and formal trousers, the yellowed gloves and patent-leather shoes. A pressed and faded rose in an envelope marked *from Adelaide Simms* brought sudden, unexpected tears to her eyes. John Malcolm Tipson. She had never known him, but he had been as real as she was. His hand had filled the silk glove her own small one slipped into so easily.

Beneath the clothing she came upon an old *Keramos* yearbook, and there he was, in the senior class of 1920: handsome, smiling, dark hair slicked back. *Jack Tipson.* Under a bundle of old issues of *Ceramic Engineering*, she found a photo of young old Lucas Henry in a crude pottery frame that looked as if it might have been made by a very small John. He had kept it. So he couldn't have *hated* his father, however much he might have blamed him for the Pelican Pottery's failure.

At the very bottom of the trunk lay a Pelican Pottery catalogue and a wooden cigar box containing brushes and modeling tools. A bottle of dried-up Gum Trag. A little booklet of gold leaf with a leaf of tissue paper between each two of gold. And a piece of polished agate shaped like a pencil with a flattish, rounded tip. For burnishing the gold onto china?

His tools. Hers now.

It was a very odd feeling. A new feeling. Not at all like the pride she had felt at the museum. That had been, *See, we weren't always nobody!* This was, in a strange, bittersweet way, a kind of sharing. Sharing the same space. When a cook and a maid had lived in the little bedrooms, he might have come up here in his sailor suit sometimes to play. He had gone down the front steps in his patent leather shoes to take Miss Adelaide Simms to the Senior Prom. Grandma. She had given him a rose for his buttonhole. And he had come home and pressed it between the leaves of a book. What book? What songs did the band play? What did she think when she saw him in his finery? What did she *feel?*

Corry sat back on her heels. Maybe Tip wondered things like that about Cordelia and Great-Grandfather. Maybe his fascination wasn't so weird after all.

If he asked again, maybe she *would* go look at his piece of Pelican pottery.

After art appreciation class on Monday, Corry waited in the hall for Tip to come out, and if he covered his surprise with an air of I-knew-you-would-come-around, he looked just plain startled and then grinned with pleasure when she said that, yes, she actually would like to see the Pelican bowl.

After school they walked down the hill in an awkward but companionable silence. Once across MacKinnon Street, Corry surprised herself by announcing out of the blue, "I'm going to make a Lotus Ware figurine," and going on to explain about the project.

Tip was enthusiastic, even envious. "It sounds great. I wish I could help. But I'm no good with my hands." He kicked a dusty, flattened cola can spinning across the road. "Sometimes I'm not sure I'm any good with my head either."

Corry looked up quickly to see whether the paper bag was on or off. Off, it seemed.

"What d'you mean?"

He couldn't mean schoolwork. He seemed to get A's with his eyes shut and his books unopened.

Tip shrugged. "Nothing much. Things just never work out the way I plan. Never have, probably never will." He darted a sideways glance at her. "Look—about telling your mother I'm a Tipson on Mother's side: When we get up to the house I want to show you something. Then you can decide for yourself whether you'll tell her. Fair enough?"

Corry was thoroughly mystified, but agreement seemed safe.

"Fair enough," she agreed.

"Do you know what 'Elysian' as in 'Elysian Way' means?" Tip asked abruptly as they closed the side door and moved into the chilly kitchen. "It's from Greek mythology: Elysium, the dwelling-place of the blessed after death. 'The abode of delight and happiness.'" He gave an odd, ironic twist to the words, so that Corry wasn't sure she should even say, "Um, interesting." And whatever it was he had meant to show her, now he seemed in no great hurry to show anything but the Pelican bowl, which sat in the middle of the kitchen table.

The bowl was a warm peach color, narrow-bottomed, with a wide, flaring rim. Across that rim and gathered at the bottom was the same drift of ivory petals that Corry had seen on the museum's Pelican plate. She picked it up and turned it over to see the small, soaring pelican stamped on the bottom as Tip crossed to the refrigerator. He opened the door and from one of the cartons stacked inside, pulled out two root beers.

"Gosh, don't you folks drink anything but root beer?" Corry blurted out. She almost added "Or eat?" since there seemed to be very little else in the refrigerator. But it was none of her business. Maybe they ate frozen dinners. Or ate out.

Tip brought a glass for Corry, but drank his own out of the bottle.

Corry set the bowl down carefully. "I think it's even nicer than the plate they have in the museum. Your mom must like it, too. To put it right out here, I mean," she added awkwardly. "Where you can all enjoy it."

Tip set his root beer down on the table. "Come here," he said shortly.

Taking Corry by the wrist, he drew her after him into the pantry, pulling the cupboard doors open as he went. Empty. Empty. Empty. Every one of them was as bare as Mother Hubbard's.

Tip crossed the back hallway and opened the door into what Corry on her first visit had supposed must be the dining room. It was empty, too. The chandelier was muffled up in a muslin bag, and on the green and ivory scenic wallpaper, green and ivory ladies and gentlemen strolled through a leafy, silent park. Sunshine falling through the sheer curtains cast bright window-pane patterns on the gleaming, naked floor.

"Come on," Tip urged. He crossed the room, his footsteps ringing loudly as he went. Baffled, Corry followed him into the front entrance hall. So they were redecorating. What was the point?

The long living-room and the smaller, bookcase-lined room beyond were empty, too. If the floors and windows, mantelpieces and bookshelves had not been so clean, it might have been eerie. But after Corry followed Tip upstairs and into one empty bedroom after another, she decided that eerie was just what it *was*. The attic was crammed full of good furniture covered with long years of dust, but below—except in the kitchen—there was not a stick of furniture anywhere. Almost as if—

"You've moved!" Corry exclaimed. She felt like a dunce. How could she be so slow? "But why are you still here if your folks and the furniture's gone? And how's come they decided to move so soon? You just *got* here. Well, almost."

"You still don't get it, do you?" Tip said glumly. He did not explain, but turned down the stairs and wordlessly led the way back through the dining room and pantry to the kitchen.

"*What* don't I get?" Corry demanded, following close behind. She was beginning to be angry. Why did he always have to make a drama out of everything? Maybe he didn't mean to make her feel stupid. But she did.

In the kitchen Tip crossed to a door next to the one

97

that led out into the side-door entryway and, turning a key in the Yale lock, opened it. "Take a look."

"Why? What's in there?" Corry asked suspiciously, remembering the doubts she had had about him on her first visit to the house.

Tip turned to give her a quizzical stare. Unexpectedly, his gloomy look vanished as he grinned.

"Don't worry. It's not Bluebeard's Chamber. Or Dr. Who's tardis."

"Doctor who's what?"

He shook his head. "Forget it. I think the room must have been the housekeeper's once upon a time."

Corry stuck her head around the doorframe and saw a small, bright room and a tiny bathroom beyond. The walls were pale yellow and the furnishings simple: an iron cot with a reading lamp and mini-TV on the nightstand beside it, a small bookcase, a straight chair, and a long, narrow table on which sat a telephone, printer, and portable computer. And several books, one of which she recognized as the textbook for the advanced-placement English class.

"This is *your* room?" Corry was frowning as she turned back into the kitchen. Then, suddenly, a number of things that had puzzled her began to make a cockeyed kind of sense. She stared at Tip in wonder.

"You're living here all by yourself. That's it, isn't it?"

Tip nodded.

"Your folks never were here, were they? So how come you are? What are you? Some kind of high-tech squatter?" She drew a deep breath. "Whose house *is* this?"

Eight

IT WAS, TIP SAID, his own house, willed to him by his grandfather, old Lucas Henry's son Christopher, Corry's great-uncle.

"Well, anyway, half-great-uncle," he amended.

He fiddled nervously with his half-empty root beer bottle. "Actually, he willed it back to Great-Grandmother in trust for me. He knew if it came straight to me, my dad would sell it and invest the money in Ruritanian uranium or IBM or kangaroo chips. He didn't want that. Grandfather was only four when he left East Liverpool, so he didn't remember it. But he loved Great-Grandfather's stories about the potteries. He always talked about coming back. He never did, though. . . ."

But he had repeated the old stories to young Tip. About the great parades when the Barnum and Bailey Circus came to town and all the potteries closed for the day. Of the pranks and adventures of the grown-up boys in the Forest and Stream Hunting and Fishing Club, the family outings to Rock Springs Park, and the time young Lucas's skiff had sprung a leak in the middle of the Ohio and he had been marooned for two hungry but adventurous days on Babbs Island. To Tip it had sounded like paradise.

After his grandfather died—when Tip was nine—he retold the tales to himself. They were about a world as different from his own as—as Kansas was from Oz. His home in New York—when he wasn't off at one boarding school or another—was a large apartment near Central Park where when he was small he had a four-foot-high stuffed elephant, a dog too tiny to hug, and magicians to entertain at his birthday parties. Later it was whole armies of miniature civil war soldiers, a life-sized figure of Yoda, and a VCR video recorder. But what he had really wanted was to go to school in New York, not New Haven or Providence. To be at home. As a kid he had worked hard at inventing pranks that would get him expelled and sent home. He gave that up after the third school. New England had more boarding schools than he had wild ideas.

His father, a corporation lawyer-executive was seldom at home anyway. You didn't make money at home. And then there came a time when his mother wasn't around to travel up to Litchfield Academy in Connecticut for Parents' Day and look more beautiful than the other mothers. She had run away. Divorced his father, married an Italian count who had no money at all, and went off to Italy to help him turn his crumbling old palazzo into a country inn.

The more Tip had thought about that, the more sensible it seemed. Not so much the running-away-from, but running-away-*to*. What if. . . .

He had laid his plans carefully, and waited. On the morning of the day his father left on a six-week business trip to the Far East, he set his plans in motion. With his modem he set up a telephone link between his computer and the company terminal in his father's office. Using the access code he had seen his father use, he typed out two letters. One, to Mr. Thurwood, the headmaster at Litchfield Academy, announced that he was withdrawing his son Lucas from Litchfield, effective immediately. Would Mr. Thurwood please send a transcript of Lucas's school records to East Liverpool High School, East Liverpool, Ohio? Sincerely, John J. Meredith. The second, addressed to "The Principal" at the high school, announced that his son, Lucas "Tip" Meredith, would be transferring from his school in Connecticut on March 1st. He would be living with his grandmother (which sounded more reasonable than "great-grandmother"), Mrs. Lawrence Dressler, of Elysian Way. Sincerely, etcetera. The office computer would print them out, and his father's secretary would sign and initial and mail them without a second thought.

When, two days later, Tip was called to Mr. Thurwood's office and given the news, he was already packed. He stowed his gear in the VW, checked that his gasoline and credit cards were in his wallet, and drove away.

Corry was wide-eyed. It was crazy. An upside-down fairy tale. A prince who wanted to be turned back into a frog?

Tip sighed. "Things went wrong from the first. I hadn't

seen Great-Grandmother since I was ten, and when Mother said she had moved back here, I thought that meant *here*-here. This house. But she was in the nursing home. From things she's said, it sounds like it was my father's idea. New York wasn't safe for dotty old ladies, and he had a plan that would make her a lot of money. She liked the sound of that, but before she got it straight in her mind what he was talking about, her New York apartment was sold and she was here. He invested the money from the apartment, and I guess he did make a lot more for her, but if she still had all her marbles, she'd be miserable. A lot of the time she's confused and thinks she's still in New York, but when she doesn't, it's awful."

Corry shook her head in disbelief. "How could your folks do that to an old lady? How old is she?"

"Only eighty-nine. At least, that's pretty young for a great-grandmother," Tip said. He added reluctantly, "But to be fair, even though my parents wanted her off their hands—she lived right across the street—I suppose they did think it would be good for her. They heard so much about Great-Grandfather's happy memories of the place from Grandfather that it probably never occurred to them she hadn't loved it too."

"So they just shipped her off into the boonies by Federal Express?" Corry was shocked.

"I don't know. They told me she had 'moved.' They must have done some checking up, though. The Birches is the best nursing home in town, and Great-Grandmother has a nice, big room, with her own furniture. I recognized most of the pieces from New York."

"But what about this house? And Mr. and Mrs. Frowd? Did you make them up?"

Tip grinned. "They're real. But the house has been rented most of the time since 1930. Mrs. Frowd says it's only been vacant since Christmas. Mr. Frowd's been the gardener for years, and Dad—because he's Great-Grandmother's 'conservator'—pays Mrs. F. to come in and dust every week until the real-estate agents find a new tenant. That's why I keep the room I'm using locked: So the real-estate agent won't see my stuff if she brings anyone around to look at the house."

Corry sat for a while, thinking.

"What if your father sends you a postcard from China or wherever? To that school in Connecticut."

"It'll be the first time," Tip said with a shrug. "And if my mother writes, they'll just forward it. They'll figure Dad didn't tell her about it."

"Then—when does your father get back?"

"April fifteenth." Tip leaned across the kitchen table. "Look, that's only two weeks from now. After the fifteenth, I'll take my chances. He'll start getting my credit-card charges on his statements about then anyhow. If his secretary notices where they're from, that's it. So just wait two weeks. Then you can tell your mother. Tell everyone."

Corry shook her head in bewilderment. "I still don't understand. What are you here *for*?"

He hesitated, and Corry saw the old, ironic look return. "Search me. I guess I came looking for the 1890s. Pretty dumb. It's—it's been like one of those dreams where you're walking along a familiar street and you turn a corner and find it's all wrong somehow. When you try to turn back, that's all changed too. You—" He broke off suddenly, his voice tight, and changed the subject. "Look, I could help with your pottery project. If you're really making your own clay and glaze, it could end up being expensive, couldn't it? I could be a—a silent partner in a new Tipson Pottery."

"No," Corry said quickly. "I have some money saved up. It'll be enough." Then, feeling guilty at the look of disappointment he quickly masked, she added, "But when I've got pieces to take up to the kiln at school, I'll need a ride."

He nodded. "It's yours. But I'd like to do more than that."

"Well—" She stood. "It's a quarter to five. My mom gets home between six and six-thirty. There's time to take that picture if you want to."

At breakfast the next morning Corry decided that after school she must go straight from the bus to Mason Color and Chemical Co. with her list of clay and glaze ingredients. If she kept putting it off, school would be out for the summer before she had even one piece ready to fire.

Her classes—even anatomy—seemed to move more slowly than a paralytic snail. When they *were* over, she was among the first to board her bus, and without Gail—who had a ride home with Scott in the Moby Dick—on hand to tease her out of it, she began to go over and over in her mind what she would say, how she would explain herself. She wished she had asked Tip to come with her.

No. On second thought, she didn't. With strangers he

might put on his superior tone, and that would alarm her into being more tongue-tied than ever.

"Somebody run over your kitty cat, lady?"

Startled, Corry looked up to find Don Chappick looming over her.

"My what?" she asked blankly.

Don sat down beside her as the bus started up and, patting her hand, explained with mock patience, "Yes, I know you don't have a kitty cat. You just looked so glum I was curious."

Corry explained about the Reggie-and-Liz project, and her errand.

"You want me to go with you?" Don asked. "Hold your clammy little hand?"

She hesitated. "Would you? Not hold my hand, I mean, but sort of—wait outside the door and whisper through the keyhole if I can't think what to say?"

Don grinned. "Like the time you got called to the principal's office in—third grade? Sure. What's this stuff you want to order?"

Corry handed him the list.

Don scanned the itemized ingredients. "One-and-a-third pounds of whiting, two and three-quarters of borax?" He looked up. "Maybe you ought to convert the fractions into ounces. It wouldn't look so Mickey-Mouse. And maybe round some of them off to the nearest half pound so they won't have to be measuring out little dribs and drabs?"

"OK." Corry fished her notebook out of her bookbag and, waiting for the bus stops so that her handwriting

105

wouldn't squiggle up and down, copied out a new list. With her head bent over the page, she never noticed Don's bemused look as he watched her write.

The color and chemical works on Second Street sat at the lower edge of the wide swath of desolation left between the river and the town after most of the Second and Third Street houses and businesses were demolished to make way for a freeway link that was still unbuilt. The building showed a windowless one-story face to the street—an unfriendly blankness that made Corry glad that Don had come along for moral support.

Inside, it was not at all what she expected. Straight ahead was a door with a sign TO THE PLANT, and glass-windowed doors to the right and left led to offices. Those to the right appeared deserted, but in a separate office at the far end of the room to the left, Corry spied a woman at a desk, telephoning. She opened the door hesitantly. Don sat down on the floor in the outer hall.

The telephone conversation did not last long, but the woman disappeared as soon as she hung up. Corry stood awkwardly, waiting, and looked around her curiously. The three desks in the outer office where she stood were deep in papers and an intriguing jumble of small vases, cups, and other objects, each apparently representing a different color or quality of glaze. Of the four chairs along the wall, the seats of two were occupied—one by two broken pitchers, the other by a handsome one of lustre ware. On one wall, above a filing cabinet, hung a painting of the lower part of town as it had looked before the demolition for the freeway.

Corry relaxed a little. She had never been in an office before except at school or the doctor's—where everything was bare and oppressively neat—and hadn't known what to expect. This wasn't half as alarming. She took a breath and walked toward the door at the far end of the office. The woman was still there, sorting through folders in a file cabinet.

"Excuse me. . . ."

The woman was first startled, then apologetic. She hadn't heard the outer door close, hadn't realized anyone was waiting. She listened politely but with a puzzled expression as Corry asked whether the company sold chemicals in small quantities and tried to explain why she needed what she needed.

"I think it's Alice you should talk to," the woman said. She dialed a number on the telephone, and when there was no answer, disappeared through a nearby door into what Corry guessed must be the plant itself, or a stockroom. Several minutes later she reappeared with a tall, middle-aged woman Corry recognized as a Mrs. Higbee, from church.

"I know you, don't I?" Mrs. Higbee asked as she gave Corry's hand a firm shake. "Cordelia—Tipson, isn't it? What can I do for you, Cordelia? Come along out here and have a seat. No, not there. The men sit there when they come out from the plant in their dusty work clothes. Over here."

She indicated a chair by the filing cabinet near the front door and sat down at the desk beside it. "Now: What is it that you need?"

Corry explained about the "old formula" and her pro-

107

posed study project without mentioning the name Lotus Ware—not really, as she had told herself before, because it would attract attention, but because making Lotus wedding-cake figures had come more and more to seem like—a little bit like making kites out of silk brocade. Kites were great, and there wasn't any reason you *shouldn't* make them out of silk brocade, but there were probably better things you could do with it.

Mrs. Higbee scanned the list. "Yes, we have most of these. The 'spar' would be feldspar. 'Whiting' is calcium carbonate. 'Regular china stain?' That was probably cobalt carbonate. Borax, yes. Lead—we don't carry white oxide of lead anymore. Only the red. But the older glazes did use red. Flint. We sell that in three different meshes."

" 'Meshes?' " Corry asked doubtfully. She had run across the word in her reading, but wasn't quite sure what it meant. "Is that a degree of—of fineness?"

Mrs. Higbee nodded. "That's right—the fineness of the screen it's sifted through. You'll want the finer five– or ten–micron flint for the clay and glaze, and the one hundred–mesh to line the frit sagger." She pointed to the note beside the frit ingredients that quoted Joshua Poole's *made in saggers and flint wash chipped off and thrown away*. "Now, you have bone ash listed here as one of the ingredients of the clay body, but we don't carry that. I'm not sure where would be the nearest place to get it. You might ask out at Hall China or over at Homer Laughlin."

"How much—" Corry ventured, twisting the strap of her bookbag into a corkscrew, "how much is the stuff you do carry going to cost?"

Mrs. Higbee considered. "Enough for a quart or two of glaze, the feldspar for the clay body and, say, three or four pounds of flint for the sagger 'wash?' " She pushed her chair back and looked at Corry over the top of her spectacles. "Well, so long as we can be sure it's just the one of you, and not a whole string of art students, there would probably be no charge."

Corry blinked. "Nothing at all?" It was a possibility that had never occurred to her.

"I think so." Mrs. Higbee smiled. "We buy the materials by the ton, so they're relatively inexpensive."

"That's great. Really great," Corry said happily. "I was really worried it would cost a lot," she confessed with a sigh of relief.

"It sounds like an interesting project. You'll have to let me know how it turns out," Mrs. Higbee said. "Do you know where you're going to get your china clay and ball clay?"

Corry shook her head. "Not yet."

"Then you might want to write to the Kentucky-Tennessee Clay Company." She went to the magazine rack at the far end of the office and flipped through a ceramics magazine. "Here it is." She read out the address and zip code.

Corry scribbled it down on the original ingredients list, and when Mrs. Higbee replaced the magazine but did not return to her desk, Corry stood up hastily and moved to the door. "When shall I. . . ."

"Why don't you come by Thursday afternoon—no, Friday would be better. We'll have the order ready for you."

Corry closed the office door sedately, but once out of view of its window she dropped her bookbag to give Don a fierce hug. "Guess what? It's going to be *free.*"

Don, who hadn't finished unfolding himself off the floor, staggered back against the wall under her weight. The loud bump made them freeze, then smother their laughter and dash for the door.

Outside, Corry announced that she was going on down to the Potters' Supply. "There's still time. You can come carry the sagger! If I'm going to have to write away and wait for the clay, I might as well use the time to make the frit for the glaze. You need a sagger for that."

"One of those big boxes made out of pottery, like in the diorama in the museum? The ones full of plates that the kiln men are loading into the kiln?"

"Not that big. Not to make six pounds of frit. Frit's glass," she explained when Don raised his eyebrows as if to say *What?* "You melt stuff down into glass, then grind it up really fine and mix it into the glaze—which gets melted into glass when you put it on your pot and fire it. I don't see why you can't just dump the frit ingredients straight into the glaze, but Joshua Poole's recipe and all the books say you have to do it the hard way. I guess there's a reason," she said doubtfully.

Corry arrived home in high spirits. The secretaries in the outer office at the Potters' Supply weren't sure whether they made a small sagger, and so had called in the sales manager. The *sales manager.* Just as if she were a regular customer: The Tipson Pottery! He had taken her out onto the plant floor to show her the standard "Rex" sagger, and with Don standing there listening, she had said with a new and unexpected confidence, "This is the smallest? It wouldn't fit in the kiln up at school. I need one about half as big."

Afterward she blushed to think how—how brisk she must have sounded. But the sales manager had actually given her a slug of the special Cordierite clay body so that she could make her own sagger and bring it back to be fired. Since it would take only half the clay of a standard sagger, they would fire it for half the price of a Rex. Ten dollars. Best of all, as he was asking questions about her project, he spotted the *North Carolina clay* on her list. "We use a North Carolina clay," he had said. "Avery clay. From Harris Mining, down in Spruce Pine. And you only need five pounds? We could give you that much. It sounds like it's in a good cause."

Don, lugging his books and the two slugs of plastic-wrapped clay the last few yards along Fourth Street, said, "Five pounds, my foot! The two together must come to more than twenty-five. Next time remind me to bring my little red wagon."

"Friday, you mean? The chemical stuff won't be very heavy," Corry said, holding the front door open. "I can carry it OK. If I come home and dump my books first."

"I don't mind," Don said hastily, almost self-consciously, as he followed her up to the attic workroom. Which was oddly unlike Don.

Corry—with dinner, homework, and mold- and sagger-making on her mind—showed him the model for the Reggie and Liz, but then took him down to the kitchen, poured him a glass of grape soda, and shooed him out across the street and home to drink it.

Corry finished her homework—even the algebra—by eight-thirty, wrote a letter to the clay suppliers, and announced that she was going up to the attic.

"If you're going to be mucking around with that clay, wear my old apron—the one with the paint stains," Mrs. Tipson said without looking up from the seam she was mending in a pair of apple-green slacks. "I don't want to have to wash that shirt and jeans again when you just put them on clean this afternoon."

The sagger proved simple to make once the clay was wedged. It was the wedging itself that presented a problem. The first loud slap of clay into the oilcloth-covered worktable made the table hop and the floorboards boom like a drum. Corry was alarmed and dismayed. Mrs. Hankins must have heard. Had to have heard. Even if she'd been asleep with cotton in her ears.

The wedging was finished on the heavy kitchen worktable, under Mrs. Tipson's disapproving eye. Only because she was so pleased with the Reggie-and-Liz model had she given in to Corry's plea. "Next time, you do it on a Saturday morning, and you warn Mrs. Hankins beforehand," she said. "Right now you scrub that up good. *Twice.*"

Back upstairs Corry divided the sagger clay, tying up one half in a double plastic bag and using the old rolling pin to roll the other half out into a sheet as near five-eighths of an inch thick—the thickness the Potters' Supply man had advised—as she could make it. Cutting out a largish circle for the bottom, she re-rolled the trimmings and the rest of the clay to make a six-inch-wide strip of the same thickness, long enough to form into a circular wall atop the circle. Following the directions in the pottery book for joining two pieces of clay, she moistened the two ends of the strip with water, scored scratchy lines on them with one of her grandfather's pointed modeling tools, and pressed them together. With her thumbs, she smoothed away the seams. She fixed the rim to the base in the same fashion. "The slab method," the book called it. She cut it free from its plaster bat with a piece of wire and stood it on another, on the smaller table, to dry.

The plaster mold was another story. Corry cut a piece from an old plastic shopping bag to protect the table, and with a hammer lightly tapped together the casting box she had made from four short boards and some nails. It might not look as professional as the one in the pottery book, but it would do.

When she had smoothed the model for Reggie-and-Liz with a scrap of fine sandpaper, she painted it and the inside of the casting box with a "sizing" of liquid soap so that the plaster wouldn't stick. Next she carefully drew its outline on a piece of stiff cardboard cut to fit snugly into the casting box, the pedestal flush with the bottom of the card. Cutting out and discarding the figure-silhouette, she shellacked and then sized the surrounding cardboard template, then bent it slightly in the middle and fitted it over the clay figures. Placing cardboard and crumpled paper in the casting box as props on which to rest the template-framed figurine, she fitted the Reginald-and-Elizabeth snugly, face-up, into the box. Then, where liquid plaster might leak through small gaps between the template and either the casting-box's walls or the figurine, she used soft clay to fill the gaps.

Plaster could be tricky, but Corry was used to mixing it. She was pouring the first half of the mold when her mother made a silent appearance on the attic stairs and pointed at her watch. Eleven o'clock.

Corry finished pouring, cleaned up, and headed happily to bed.

Nine

CORRY, SEARCHING through her pockets for her key when she arrived home Wednesday, turned and saw Mr. Hankins on his way back from the neighborhood market with a grocery bag on each arm. She waited to open the door for him.

"Oh, and I'm sorry about the banging last night," she said with a blush when she had told him about the visits to Mason Color and Chemical and the Potters' Supply. "I was wedging clay. I thought it would be OK because your bedroom's in the back, but it made the table jump right off the floor."

"Yes, if you're using an ordinary table, I suppose it would," Mr. Hankins said. "My friend Albert's work counter was heavy and actually attached to the wall. But there's no need to worry about last night. We had the television on in the bedroom—the Fred Astaire special—and didn't hear a thing. We did hear you shifting furniture on Saturday, though. I take it you've made yourself a workplace up there."

Corry nodded. "You'll have to come see it," she said hastily, wishing she had thought to ask him before. She really should have.

He beamed. "I would like to very much. And," he added happily as he started up the stairs, "you might just have a use for two good two-quart crocks with lids that I kept from my decorating and glazing days. Doris has always been afraid to use them for making her pickles or sauerkraut. Too many of the glazes I stored in them contained lead. She doesn't trust them to be safe."

"If you're sure you can't use them," Corry said. "That'll be great. I'll be going up in about five minutes."

There was no mail. As Corry changed from her baggy man's sweater and patchwork skirt into her oldest jeans and tied on the paint-stained apron she told herself that it was at least a week—perhaps two—too soon to expect an answer from the clay suppliers. But if her letter *could* reach them by tomorrow. . . .

Mr. Hankins was already out waiting on the upstairs landing with a bulging shopping bag in his arms when she headed for the stairs. He had put in his old broad-bottomed bowl for glaze-dipping, too. As Corry showed off the new attic studio, he inspected everything with great interest. He handled Grandpa John's modeling tools lovingly.

"How pleased he would be to know you were using these! An excellent man, your grandfather. I knew him only after the Pelican Pottery's troubles began. It was at that time that he divided the house into the two apartments in hopes that the rent would keep his family afloat. Every other penny went back into the pottery. But even with all his worries then, and after his troubles had broken him down, he encouraged Albert and me in our little hobby. He was always more an artist than a businessman," he said with a sigh as he went on to the second table.

Corry would have liked to ask about her father—what was he like before he went off to Vietnam? When he was a little boy. When—but even though she ached to know, she shied away from asking. If she was shy of asking her mother, it seemed somehow disloyal to ask anyone else.

Mr. Hankins approved the sagger, agreeing that it should certainly be dry enough to take down to the Potters' Supply on Friday afternoon. After all, it would almost certainly not be fired before Monday. He admired the mold— and though it had no keys (What were they? Corry wondered), the slight V-shape of the division between the halves would help to keep the inner faces of the two parts from sliding out of alignment.

Best of all, he was able to answer Corry's questions about the making of the frit. The "flint wash" was a dried paste of water and ground-up flint coating the inside of the sagger so that the frit, when it was melted into glass, would not weld to it so firmly that it could be broken free of the sagger. When it *was* melted, it must be taken out of the kiln hot and plunged into water. That, he explained, fractured the frit so that it might more easily be broken up into splinters. Otherwise, you would have a long, hard job with a hammer. As for removing the sagger from the mass of glass it contained, that was simple: Find a concrete floor or pavement—and drop it.

Corry grinned. "But after you've got it all into splinters and washed them off, how do you grind it?"

"In a ball mill." The old man pulled at his lower lip thoughtfully. "For all I know, potteries nowadays might use commercial frits, but there must be ball mills around still. Dear me, I wonder what happened to Albert's father's little one. The one we used. Never mind. You might try out at Hall China. Ask whether they would grind a small batch."

Corry made a face. *More* strangers to talk to.

After dinner Corry finished the mold. Carefully turning over the casting box, she threw away the crumpled paper and the cardboard template, sized the surfaces—the inner face of the front mold and the back of the figurine—onto which she would pour the plaster for the second half, mixed a fresh batch, poured it, and got to bed early for a change.

The next morning, she tiptoed up to the attic to take the box apart and inspect the mold. Perfect! The halves came apart easily, and though for a moment it seemed as if the clay model wanted to stick fast in the front half, a little gentle pressure lifted it free.

And the day looked like being as good as its beginning.

"I'll take you down to Hall China," Tip said at lunch. "I brought the car because I promised to go see Great-Grandmother. If you like, I'll take you to the Potters' Supply and that other place tomorrow, too."

"You don't have to," Corry said. "Don's going with me.

But it'd be great if we could go down to Hall China after school. If I get the frit made next week, I'll be ready to mix up the glaze whenever I need it, and as soon as the other bit of clay comes, I can really get going."

"Don Chappick?" Tip seemed startled.

Corry nodded as she started on her chicken patty. Tip had fallen silent, but she didn't notice. In her mind she was already rehearsing what she would say to whomever at Hall China. She needed to ask where to send for bone ash, too. She had almost forgotten that.

Tip finished his chicken patty and apple crisp without saying a word.

The receptionist at Hall China, mistaking Corry and Tip for visitors come to take the pottery tour, explained that they were too late. They would have to come back tomorrow. Earlier in the afternoon. Corry's explanation of her errand seemed only to confuse the young woman, and Corry —flustered by Tip's look of polite attention—tried again.

"A ball mill?" the young woman asked. "I'm not sure —I think you want to talk to Mr. Tremont. He's back in the lab. If you follow the tour arrows along to the second group of vending machines, it's the door right there. Just follow the tour arrows." She pointed to a doorway around to her right.

Mr. Tremont was a short, round, cheerful man with bright, sharp eyes. "An old formula, eh? Soft-paste porcelain? Sounds interesting. Mind telling me how old, or are you keeping that under your hat?" Seeing Corry's cheeks redden, he smiled. "Now you've got me really curious. Tell you what: We'll mill your frit for you—no charge—if you'll come out to show us the finished product. Bargain? Oh, and here's that address for the bone ash."

When Corry had copied it, she thanked Mr. Tremont with a shy smile. When she reached the front entrance, she was still smiling—until she turned around and discovered that she had lost Tip.

He reappeared a moment later.

"I was watching some of the work," he explained. "When is Mrs. Giorgiadis taking the class on that pottery tour? May? I hope I'm still here."

"I thought you were kind of quiet in there. Even for you," Corry said when he had unlocked the car door for her. "Were you thinking about Great-Grandpa and the potteries, too?"

"What? Oh. Yes, in a way." Tip hesitated, his hand on the ignition key. "Corry? Will you come with me to visit Great-Grandmother?"

"Me?" Corry looked alarmed. "Why?"

Tip looked carefully both right and left as he pulled out of the parking-lot drive, and in doing so, managed neatly to avoid meeting her eyes. "I want to try to find out more about Great-Grandfather," he said. "You'd be interested in that. And I'd like you to meet her. Even when she was young, she must have been worlds different from Cordelia."

"But you like her, don't you?" Corry was puzzled by something in his tone. "You must, if you thought you were coming here to live with her."

"I love her," Tip said slowly, as if the words were hard to say straight out. "But—'like?' I'm not sure. Funny. What I remember most about her are things that aren't really *her*. The platterful of bacon at breakfast when I stayed overnight with her, the wonderful birthday toys from England and Germany—even the way she smelled. Like lilies and lilac. But I don't really know anything about her—where she was from, whether she liked to dance or play the bassoon, or went to Sunday school or college or—I just don't know."

The Birches, the nursing home, was a large, Victorian house with two tall weeping-birch trees to flank the front walk, and flowerbeds massed with daffodils just beginning to bloom. There were bright-cushioned wicker chairs on the front porch and gold-framed mirrors and fresh flower arrangements in the quiet front hall. Three old ladies and an old man sat in a book-lined library room off to the right, playing cards and drinking tea. Corry guessed that it must cost—well—a *lot* to live there. She had gone with Gail once to visit her grandmother at *her* nursing home. Old Mrs. Mestrovic had moved out of Gail's parents's house in a huff after an argument and ended up in a tiny room without a closet in a house without carpets, where the old folks sat around in their slippers watching the dust settle. Here the carpets might not be new, but they were beautiful. Orientals, Corry thought they were called. She wasn't sure where that meant they were from.

"She's forgotten I was coming," Tip murmured, "or she'd be down here waiting. It's probably a New York day."

121

He led the way upstairs and along the hall to a door bearing a small enameled nameplate that read *Gwendolyn Dressler*, and knocked.

The door was opened by a very thin old lady—taller than Corry had expected—carefully made up, with thin, penciled eyebrows and wearing a pale green suit and pearls. She peered at them and then clapped her beringed hands together in delight.

"Sandy! How lovely!" she quavered. "And you've brought a friend. Oh, do come in off the doorstep, my dears. Come in!" Her voice, thready as it was, had great charm.

As old Mrs. Dressler turned back into the room, Tip leaned down to whisper in Corry's ear, "Sandy's short for Alexander—my grandfather. But don't worry. It's OK."

Corry looked around her in awe. It was, as Tip had said, a lovely room. So long as you didn't look out the window, she thought, it wouldn't be at all hard to believe you were in New York. There was a carpet with a raised design, all ivory and blues, and ivory-colored chairs with carved, curved legs and pretty needlework seats and backs. The other furniture was either of walnut or the same ivory color, and the walls were papered with a pale, textured cloth. Seen close-to, it appeared to be made of fine, woven grasses. Several paintings, all flower studies, hung in just the right places, at just the right height. There was even a fireplace with gleaming andirons and an ivory-painted mantelpiece. A mirror in a wide, gold-edged, carved walnut frame hung over it. In the far corner a canopy bed hid behind silk curtains.

"Come sit down, dear." Tip's great-grandmother patted

the place beside her on the settee. "And introduce me to your young friend."

"This is Corry, Great-Grandmother," Tip said, so quickly that the old lady seemed not to miss hearing a family name. "Corry's interested in Lotus Ware, and I brought her along to see your prize piece."

Mrs. Dressler looked as startled as Corry. "Lotus Ware? Have I a prize piece? Are you sure, dear?

Tip crossed to a glass-fronted cabinet that held a few leatherbound books, two pairs of figurines of dainty old-fashioned shepherdesses, and a collection of delicate porcelain cups and saucers. He opened one of the lower doors.

"This," he said, bringing to the coffee table a small, round, white globe of a vase. "It's not marked, but it is Lotus. You remember, Corry. There's one like it in the museum."

Corry knelt on the carpet, the better to see without touching the delicate porcelain. If there had been one in the museum, she had missed seeing it. She could not have forgotten it. Instead of having a circular opening at the top, the eggshell-thin clay had been pierced and cut into a simple lacework of leaves. A few small, white berries were the only added decoration. Corry reached out, but then drew back her hand.

"It's lovely!"

"Do you think so? If I had known it was Lotus Ware, I would have gotten rid of it long ago," the old lady said testily, turning to Tip. "Sandy, your father may go on and on about his blessed Lotus Ware, but I have never been able to see what the fuss was about. It's all quite overrated. Some pieces have as much elegance as a washerwoman in a Lily Daché hat."

She reached out her hand for the little vase, but Tip distracted her by asking whether she was still having trouble sleeping. He replaced the vase in the cupboard while she answered and Corry returned to her chair.

"No, dear. No trouble at all. I think your father must have given Mrs. Mollis a few days off, because when I ring the bell at night now for my hot chocolate, a very nice young woman brings me a pill with it. I don't remember her name. . . ."

Her voice trailed off on a note of confusion, and when Tip sat down again beside her, she leaned close to whisper in his ear. "Who is that young person? Has she come to collect for the Heart Association?"

"That's Corry, Great-Grandmother. She's a friend of mine. I brought her to see your porcelain."

"Did you dear? I do forget sometimes." She looked at Tip archly. "Only a 'friend?' Are you sure?"

Corry blushed fiercely. To her surprise Tip did too. His great-grandmother patted his knee. "Only teasing, my dear. Would you two young things like a cup of tea?"

"Yes, please. May I help?" Tip asked as the old lady crossed to the tea cart by the fireplace.

"No, dear. I think it must be Mrs. Mollis's day off, but she always leaves the tea things ready, and this nice little electric kettle."

When the water had boiled and the tea was steeping, Tip ventured, "Why was Great-Grandfather always 'going on about' Lotus Ware?"

"Was he?" the old lady asked vaguely as she sat down again. "Will you bring the cart over here, dear?"

"You said he was," Tip urged as he wheeled the cart to her side.

The old lady sat with her hands limp in her lap. "Said he was what?" she asked in distress.

Tip took one of her hands and squeezed it reassuringly. "Why was Great-Grandfather always talking about Lotus Ware?"

Old Mrs. Dressler freed her hand and reached for the teapot. "I suppose because when Knowles, Taylor and Knowles was rebuilt after their fire, he worked for three years with that Poole person making Lotus Ware. It wasn't profitable, you know. An expensive waste of time. So it was discontinued."

Corry was so surprised—and excited—that when Mrs. Dressler offered her sugar for her tea, she spilled her sugar cubes onto the floor.

Mrs. Dressler waved her hand. "Never mind. The maid will get them later." But when the old lady turned back to Tip, Corry searched underfoot and scooped them up. She put them on her saucer.

Mrs. Dressler had apparently slipped a gear at some point, for suddenly she addressed Tip as 'Tip.'

"Tip, dear, I'm afraid your great-grandfather never quite got the clay out from under his fingernails. No matter where we were—in a fine restaurant or at an important dinner party—he turned the plates over to have a look at the pottery mark. And Lotus! You would think it was Belleek or Dresden. It was very tiresome of him."

125

"But—" Corry blurted out, "what did he *do* at K.T. and K.? Did he work with clay, or decorate, or what?"

Old Mrs. Dressler, who had already forgotten that Corry was there, peered at her uncertainly. Reaching into her suit pocket, she drew out a pair of eyeglasses and fumbled them on.

For a moment she only stared. Then, alarmingly, her face crumpled up as if she would weep. "No, no. Go away. *Please* go away," she whispered.

Ten

ORRY SAT QUIETLY in the wide front hallway, waiting for Tip to come down from his great-grandmother's room. First startled, then confused and hurt, she had fled down the stairs past the attendant going up in answer to the buzzer from Mrs. Dressler's room.

But the tears that came were angry ones. Tip should have *known* her resemblance to Cordelia might alarm the old lady. Or guessed. When he appeared fifteen minutes later, Corry got up and went to the door in silence. But once they were outside, she stopped and turned accusingly.

"Did you explain to her? About who I am? So she wouldn't think I was Great-Grandma's ghost?"

"Yes—at least, that you were some kind of cousin," he said uncomfortably. "She did calm down, and the nurse gave her some kind of pill."

"I shouldn't have come. It *was* because I look like Great-Grandma, wasn't it?"

Tip nodded. "But I think it was your asking about Great-Grandfather's work—about the Lotus Ware—that set her off. Then after she had a good look at you, I think she really may have taken you for a ghost. After you left, and she calmed down a little, she said, 'She haunted me all those years. All those years. But why now? Why now?'"

Corry gave him an angry look and went on down the steps to the sidewalk and the car. "She threw the cup at the painting of Great-Grandma, didn't she? And you figured she did, but she wouldn't answer questions, so you thought up a little experiment, didn't you? Give her a little push with a piece of Lotus and Great-Grandma's face. An experiment. With that nice old lady!"

"You mightn't think she was all that nice if you heard some of the names she called Cordelia," Tip snapped. "And how was I to know she had a real 'thing' about her?"

"I guess you couldn't," she admitted as the VW squealed away from the curb. "But if half the time she doesn't even know what year it is, you could've guessed it would at least confuse her. You *could've* explained who I was right off."

"I didn't. I'm sorry."

His face was calm, even pleasant, but Corry could tell that he was upset. Angry, even.

"What names?" she asked after a moment, holding onto the dashboard as the car made a tight downhill turn.

"It's not important. She was upset."

"I want to know. What names?"

Tip drew a deep breath. "OK. 'That drunkard-potter's daughter,' for one. A common factory-hand. 'That frizzle-haired little witch'—at least, I think it was 'witch.' Enough?"

"Yes." Corry said. She leaned her forehead against the cold glass of the window and watched the Travelers Hotel slip by. "You know—"

What?"

"I was just thinking. Great-Grandpa must have loved them both very much. He never forgot my great-granny, or he wouldn't have taken her portrait and her things to his new house, and yours wouldn't've been—wouldn't *be*—so jealous. And he had to love yours, because he gave up the potteries and went away with her to live in New York when he'd rather have stayed. It's funny. They must've been so—different."

Tip looked across at her as they waited for the traffic light. "Spellbinders both," he said.

Corry was not listening. "You know—" She turned to him. "You've got to tell your folks how miserable she is here when she knows she's here. There've got to be nice places in New York that take good care of old people. Where they get to go out sometimes to plays and art shows and stores with pretty things. She could afford it, couldn't she? You've *got* to get her back there."

"I will." Tip gave the words the weight of a promise. He smiled. "You know, you're really something. Frizzle-haired Little Witch the Second, in fact." He reached out to ruffle her hair.

Corry batted his hand away. "Anyhow, we did find out something important. About Great-Grandpa, I mean. He could've actually *made* the Lotus cup. He could have, couldn't he?" She frowned. "What's the matter?"

Tip pulled up at the curb behind Mr. Chappick's old Chrysler. "I think," he said, turning up his collar and scrunching down in his seat, "you have an unwelcoming committee."

"Clown!" Corry looked across the street and saw that the committee was her mother, watching them with a frown from the front porch. "Oh, no! It's Thursday. Mom's day off. I completely forgot. She's probably been tapping her foot like that for the last hour."

She opened the car door, snatched up her bookbag, and scrambled out. "Thanks for taking me to Halls'," she called back as she crossed the street. "See you tomorrow."

"About time!" Mrs. Tipson turned to finish hosing the sudsy water off the front porch and turned the nozzle to shut off the spray. "Who was that?" she asked curiously. "I couldn't see."

"Tip Meredith. He's in a couple of my classes. He took me down to Hall China to ask about getting the frit-glass ground up for the glaze, and about where I can get bone ash." It was the truth, but not enough of it, and it had an ashen taste.

"That was nice of him." Mrs. Tipson watched the trim little car move slowly toward the corner at Monroe Street. "Next time you oughta ask him in. Have some soda pop and a piece of cake."

"Maybe," Corry said, and then laughed. "Sometime when we've got root beer. That's what he likes."

"You like him?"

Corry watched her mother watch the little car around the corner and out of sight. "He's OK," she said, suddenly cautious.

"He ask you out?"

"Nope."

Mrs. Tipson gave up and turned her attention back to the porch. "I guess this'll do. How about I take your books in and you go turn the hose off and loop it up on the hanger? I got something I want to talk to you about. In the kitchen."

Something—a shift in her tone of voice?—made Corry uneasy. When she had coiled the garden hose and coiled it onto the wooden bracket at the side of the house, she went to hang up her jacket in the hall and pushed through the swinging door into the kitchen.

The glossy color booklet from the Harlan Hotel Trades Institute lay on the table.

"I got a start on spring cleaning today," Mrs. Tipson said as she turned the fire on under a skillet. She added margarine and began slicing onions into it. "I turned out and washed all these cupboards, washed the bedroom curtains. And I turned your mattress. I think you better tell me what that thing there's about."

Corry drew a deep breath. In her enthusiasm for making the Reggie-and-Lizzes she had completely forgotten about the pastry-cook course. She hadn't given it a thought for a week.

"I'm waiting."

"I wanted to find out how you get to be a master pastry cook," Corry said, and then plunged in at the deep end. "I told you: I wanted us to live in Pittsburgh and have our own shop, and make April's Cakes famous. I'd need to know how to bake a lot more *kinds* of cakes and pastries than you do now, though. I figured that meant I'd have to go to cooking school. Mrs. Eckert said Harlan was the best for what I wanted. And it's right on the bus line that goes past Aunt June's. I could stay there. . . ."

Mrs. Tipson listened with her arms folded. Corry, as she continued, thought she saw a flicker of interest. But where that should have encouraged her, she found an odd little twinge of unease.

". . . and then if you didn't want to sell the house because of the Hankinses, you could rent out our part, and we could rent the other half of Aunt June and Uncle Russ's place."

Mrs. Tipson frowned. "That's all pie in the sky, and you know it."

"No," Corry said doggedly. "I don't know it." But why then had she used the past tense? *I wanted us to live in Pittsburgh*. She held her breath and waited for the fireworks.

"Besides," he mother said slowly, "those Barneses rent the other half of Russ and June's duplex. With three kids, they're probably set to stay. And where would you sleep while you were there going to school? Your Aunt June's sewing room? Granny's in the guest room."

"It's got twin beds," Corry reminded her. But the thought slid into her mind that there wouldn't be much sleep to be had in Granny Binney's room. Granny had a nervous habit of clicking her teeth in her sleep, and just when you were finally dropping off, she switched to snoring. How could she have forgotten?

"That'd last about three weeks," Mrs. Tipson said drily as she tore up the booklet. "Come off it, Corry."

Corry steeled herself to fight back tears. There was no use arguing. Even if Granny and Aunt June agreed, neither would be able to budge her mom once she'd dug in her heels. Maybe it had all been pie—cake?—in the sky. Maybe there was nothing to do but give up and start hoping for a job as a school secretary. Or receptionist in a doctor's office. That way, at least she wouldn't have to wrestle with math.

"What's for dinner?" she asked, shifting ground. She tried for a light tone and was surprised that her voice didn't tremble. And that there were no tears to fight back. More perplexing still was the queer, elusive feeling of relief that niggled at her under the disappointment. When she tried to identify it, it skittered away like a silvery drop of mercury she couldn't put her finger on.

With her homework finished and nothing more to be done on the Reggie-and-Lizzes until the replies to her letters about the clays and bone ash came, Corry felt lost. After fifteen minutes of the last act of a television mystery she could make neither head nor tail of, she left her mother half asleep in front of the TV and went to her bedroom. She returned with the photo of the painted Lotus cup and the box of bits and pieces.

Idly, she began to try to fit them together. It seemed a hopeless job. In even the nastiest jigsaw puzzles there were knobs and sockets, or whatever you called them, to be fitted together. Simple. Either they fit or they didn't. But the edge of one thin shard of porcelain might seem to fit against several others. The splintered bits seemed hopeless. A few were too fine to handle even with tweezers, and where they had come from was anyone's guess. The only clue for the larger pieces was the delicately ridged seashell texture on the exterior of the cup's bowl that sworled from its base to the rim. By matching on two pieces the lines of its small, smooth ripples, she was finally able to fit together two small parts of the rim.

But what to do next? Ordinary white squeeze-bottle glue wouldn't hold for long. Not on porcelain. It wasn't porous enough. But if you used epoxy, and made a mistake, you were stuck with it.

Stuck with it. Corry found herself smiling at the unconscious pun and wondered what was wrong with her. It was pathetic: Up until 5:30, she had thought she had the future under control. Or at least pretty well organized. And now that it had all gone into the wastebasket with the shredded booklet, here she was, grinning at silly non-jokes when she ought to be depressed. She tried to be, picturing herself working at a desk in a fluorescent-lit office. At a computer terminal in a—a travel agency, entering the wrong code numbers and sending Mrs. Who to Cairo, Egypt, instead of Cairo, Illinois, and Mr. Soandso to Hong Kong when his mother was expecting him in Cleveland. Awful for Mrs. Who and Mr. Soandso.

Or maybe not.

It was no good. All she could do was giggle.

•   •   •

On Friday afternoon Corry and Don dropped the sagger off to be fired and collected the glaze materials. Afterward Don came up to the attic to hang the pigeonhole box on the wall for her. But when she had labeled nine of the pigeonholes and tucked the plastic bags of chemicals away, there was nothing more to be done. Corry felt suddenly anxious. With spring break the coming week, if the ball clay and bone ash didn't arrive, all that wonderful free time would go to waste.

"Would you like to go to a movie tonight?" Don asked offhandedly, picking up the model of the Reggie-and-Liz for a closer look.

"Sure. What's on?" Corry looked around the attic room. She would have to find a pan or bowl for mixing the frit ingredients. . . .

"Um, *Rinky-dink* at the American, and *The Drama Club* and *Netherworld* out at Calcutta. Pop said I could have the car. We could go out for a pizza or something after." Replacing the model on the table, he remarked, "You made them smaller than your old pair. How's come?"

"Smaller? No, they're the same. Five inches, counting the pedestal."

"If you say so," Don shrugged as he followed her to the stairs.

Corry frowned, and turned back for a look. Odd. They did look a bit smaller. She took up the piece of yardstick and measured. Just under four and three-quarters inches. For a moment she stood frowning at the figurine. Then she groaned.

"Dumb, dithering *idiot*. Of course! It's shrunk. The

135

books *said* clay shrinks when it dries and when it's fired. I just didn't listen. *Spit!*"

"What's the big deal?" Don was surprised. "They still look fine."

"Oh, sure," Corry said despairingly. "And when I cast the real ones in the mold, they'll shrink even more when they dry because bone china just does. And when *they're* fired, too. They'll end up having to go on wedding cakes for midgets."

"You mean you've got to start all over again?"

Corry nodded angrily. "Yes. But the plaster's all gone, and I don't think I've got enough left of the clay Mrs. Giorgiadis gave me."

"Good." Don was relieved. "Then you can't start tonight. I mean, it's rotten luck, but a movie'll take your mind off it. Which one do you want to go see? When I get home, I'll phone about the times."

Corry considered. "I've seen *The Drama Club. Netherworld*, I guess. There was this neat dragon in the preview I saw on TV. I'd really like to know how they *do* that stuff."

"You mean they don't use real dragons? OK, OK! No hitting! But you thought they did in *Dragonlord.* Admit it."

"I was seven when I fell for that one. You're the only one who still thinks it's funny." She glared.

"Cross my heart, I'll never mention it again." He made an X on his T-shirt." And tomorrow I'll take you where you can get as much clay as you want—for free," he promised with a grin.

. . .

Corry knelt in the tussocky grass and peered over the bank of the narrow trickle of the stream that cut through Don's uncle's farm while Don, wearing his cousin's high rubber boots, stood in the water and dug another chunk of yellow clay from the bankside.

"It seems funny to have it come from someone's farm instead of from a company," Corry said. "But I guess a hundred and fifty years ago it would have seemed funny the other way around. You know, it would really be neat to copy that wonderful mug in the museum. The one with the frog in it? It was made with this kind of clay. Here, give me that chunk. It's the best yet. There's not as much gritty-looking stuff in it."

"My aunt used to fool around with it. Making flower pots, things like that. She said to tell you she mixes it up with water into—'slip?'—into whatever you call it, and then squeezes it through a piece of nylon to get the crud out."

Corry nodded. "I know. And to get it thick again, you let it settle, and keep pouring the water off the top. Then I'll wedge however much I need in with what's left over from the school clay."

As Don shoveled the last chunk out onto the grass and stepped up from the stream bed, Corry wound her arms around him in a hug. "This was a great idea, Donny. Thanks."

Don squeezed back happily and gave a mournful sigh when she pulled free. "If I dig some more, can I have another?"

"Clown!" Corry laughed as she scooped the two best

chunks of clay into the plastic grocery bag she had brought along. "I'll race you back to the farmhouse."

The whole of spring break seemed like that to Corry—swinging daffily between disaster and serendipity, miscalculation and almost-magical solutions.

Corry watched every day for the mailman, but no letter came from the clay company. Then Mrs. Tipson, while cleaning the cupboard under the stairs, found Granny Tipson's old kitchen scales, so the problem of weighing the glaze and clay ingredients was solved before Corry had even thought about it.

On Monday Mrs. Tipson produced the money for a fresh supply of plaster of Paris, and Corry made two larger bats.

The new model—even clearer in detail since it was an inch taller and that much easier to work with—was finished and dry by Tuesday.

The sagger was fired on Tuesday and ready for pickup at the Potters' Supply on Wednesday. Once Corry had coated it inside with a paste of powdered flint and water, and the paste had dried, it took only minutes to combine and mix the frit ingredients—borax, feldspar, flint, whiting, and china clay—and fill the sagger ready for firing. But—no school until Monday, no kiln.

When Mr. Hankins next visited the attic workroom to see what progress she was making, Corry was so intent on fashioning tiny practice clay roses with an old small-size pastry bag and a No. 6 decorating tube that when the old gentleman cleared his throat as if to say "Excuse me," she jumped in fright—and knocked the original model of Reggie-and-Liz to the floor. With the mold made, she had no more use for it, but it was sad to see poor Reggie beheaded.

But then Mr. Tremont from the lab at Hall China phoned later in the afternoon to say that he had heard from his friend Ralph Ginger, who had heard it from *his* friend George Hankins, that Corry was ready to melt her frit. If she could bring her sagger out to the plant, he would fire it in the lab's small kiln.

Even that piece of good fortune could have ended in disaster. But Tip had shown up in the VW as Don, weak from laughter—and Corry from shrieks of alarm—were setting out for the River Road and the East End on Corry's father's and Don's bicycles, with the sagger swaying dangerously in a carton-cradle slung between them. They went, all three, in the VW instead. Corry, who an hour earlier had come home to find a letter from the Ceramic Color and Chemical Company saying "I am sending you a sample of ten pounds of bone ash—Good luck with your project," was too elated to notice that Tip never said a word to Don, or Don to Tip.

Two white plastic bucket-style tubs of bone ash were delivered by a parcel-service truck on Thursday. But still no clay from Kentucky. Tip appeared in mid-afternoon with three tubes of China-Fix he had ordered from New York, and a bunch of daffodils and tulips from the garden on Elysian Way for Mrs. Tipson. To Corry's surprise, her mother produced a quart bottle of root beer from the fridge.

139

And when Tip invited Corry to go Lotus-hunting in Lisbon and Salem on Saturday, her mother said, "Don't be silly, hon. Sure you've got time."

But on Friday Corry wished she'd said no. A Mr. Franz phoned to explain that he was the local representative of the Kentucky-Tennessee Clay Company, and that her letter had been referred to him. Would she be in between five-fifteen and five-thirty? He would be on his way home from the Homer Laughlin plant, and could drop her clay off then if it would be convenient. *If!*

Don came over after supper. Corry carefully weighed out on Grandma Tipson's old kitchen scales the ash and feldspar and powdered clay. Don carried a plastic bucket of water up from downstairs, and settled down cheerfully to stir as Corry poured in the ingredients. It was while he stirred that he asked whether Corry would like to go to the Pirates game two weeks from tomorrow. And maybe dinner after, at a real restaurant? Corry was surprised. But it did sound like fun. She had never seen any live baseball game, let alone a pro game. And the closest thing to a "real" restaurant she had ever been in was the Pizza Hut.

But then, when the clay was mixed, strained into the big crock and left to settle, and when they had tiptoed down the stairs so they wouldn't disturb the Hankinses, and when Don had washed his hands and pulled on his sweater and had the door open ready to go home, he bent and kissed Corry goodnight.

It was only a peck. And more on the cheek than the corner of her mouth, even. But he had never kissed her before. Not even a brotherly smack. Hugs, yes. But always

Teddy-bear hugs. Or at least— As she closed and bolted the door, Corry remembered how slow he had been to let her go, down by the stream on his uncle's farm where they dug the clay.

"If I dig some more, can I have another?"

"Clown!"

And now asking her for a real date.

Maybe he hadn't been clowning. Not really. Not underneath. Corry felt a wave of dismay, as if she'd lost her footing in a sea-swell. Dismay and alarm and a frightening sense of loss. Ever since she could remember, Don had been around when she needed him. And gone when she didn't. Kind, unflappable, funny. Accepting her quirks and fears. Never—needing. This felt a little like being swept downriver in an open boat, in a current too swift for her oars. Half an hour later she found herself watching the end of *Dallas* in the living room, where her mother had moved the TV with the arrival of warmer weather. She didn't remember coming in from the hall, let alone what had happened on the screen.

She was a long time falling asleep, but slid over the edge at last, mumbling, "No, Don likes Angie, Don likes Angie . . ." like an incantation.

Eleven

BY BREAKFAST THE NEXT morning Corry decided that if she *hadn't*
imagined the change in Don, maybe it would go away if
she ignored it.

Tip arrived at ten, and Corry came out to the car wearing an old puff-sleeved blouse and paisley shawl from one
of the attic trunks with her window-curtain skirt, and boots.
From the corner of her eye she saw the living-room curtain
twitch, and knew that her mother was watching. And probably still muttering, "He'll think you look like an ad for a
thrift shop!" Which wasn't really fair, considering that
snapshots of pretty April Binney in her senior year when
she was one of the Pottery Queen's court, showed her in
sandals, headband, beads, and a long, sacklike dress with
the hem slashed like buckskin fringe.

Tip grinned. "You look great. If the skirt was even

longer and you had one of those wide, flattop hats with ribbon or tulle, you'd be Cordelia setting out for a picnic. I like it."

They spent the morning on country roads and in antique shops. The only piece of china they came across that bore the Lotus Ware mark on its bottom was a cupless saucer. Corry saw two small, plain vases, one green and one plum-colored, sisters to a dark blue one on the Hankins's mantelpiece, but they were three dollars each. The plum-colored one would have been lovely beside the blue. She might have splurged the dollar she had in her pocket, but not three.

The morning's only real find was a small, curly, nicely silly-looking china sheep. It appeared to be quite old and was just the size of those old Mrs. Dressler's shepherdesses tended. To Corry's amazement, Tip paid sixty dollars for it and seemed to think it a great bargain.

"It's lovely, but I don't suppose it's Dresden. No such luck," he said. "Great-Grandmother will know. It does look as if it *might* belong with Bo and Peep."

At one o'clock, when Corry had for half an hour been looking longingly at every restaurant and snack bar they passed, Tip announced that he had brought a picnic.

"That's what's under the tarpaulin in back. And I know just where we ought to eat it."

"Where's that?" Corry asked. She unfastened her safety belt and twisted around to lift a corner of the plastic-coated sheeting from what seemed far too large a hump for a picnic lunch. Underneath sat a large wicker case more like a miniature steamer trunk than a picnic basket.

"You'll see. I found it last week. It shouldn't be more than half an hour from here."

"I don't think I'll last that long," Corry objected. "Can't I lift up the lid and sneak half a sandwich?"

"The food's not on top. You can't get to it without unpacking the whole works," Tip cautioned. "Don't worry. It's worth waiting for. You'll survive. Think about—the U.S. Postal Service."

Corry stared as she clicked her safety belt shut again. "How's come?"

"Vibrations. Concentration of telepathic force. *Deliver letter from clay company. Deliver clay,*" he intoned.

"Oh, no," she exclaimed. "It's come. I forgot to tell you. This really nice man from the clay company *brought* it. Don and I mixed it up last night."

Tip was silent for a moment. "And you're here instead of at home and up to your elbows in it? Should I be flattered?"

"Not exactly." Corry grinned. "I can't really do much but pour the water off the top as the clay settles, and when it's solid enough, dry it out even more on bats. At least, not until I've made the new mold. I thought that to make the slip—the liquid clay you pour into a mold—I could just use the soupy clay, but one of the books I've been reading says that kind of slip shrinks too much, and warps. There's this chemical with a weird name you mix in so you use hardly any water at all. 'Water-glass,' it's called. I need to find out how much it costs, and maybe get some today. At a hardware store. We were parked right by one in Lisbon, but I forgot."

144

"We pass one on the way home," Tip said shortly.

It was a while before he spoke again. Then it was to ask, almost formally, "How are you going to get your Reggie-and-Lizzes fired once they're cast? Jeff Weir says his Art IV class is doing only one more firing. And they use a low-firing clay. Doesn't the kiln have to be a lot hotter for bone china?"

Corry noticed his politely conversational tone, but thought nothing of it. "About twenty-three hundred degrees Fahrenheit. Something like that. Mrs. Giorgiadis was going to check up on how to run the kiln so she can do the two firings for me. 'Bisque' first and then one for the glaze. Since it's sort of 'preliminary research' for a real project next year, she says it's OK to use the school kiln."

"Um," Tip said.

Corry fell silent. She wondered uncertainly whether the "um" was supposed to mean something, but then decided that he had only asked just to be saying something. It always seemed to happen. Every time she began to feel really comfortable around her cousin, the paper bag reappeared.

As they turned off onto a narrower road, winding their way through rolling farms and woodland, Tip woke from his preoccupation. He sat forward a little, half hunched over the wheel, and began to watch the roadsides.

"Where *are* we going?" Corry asked.

"You don't know? You've never been out here?" Tip gave her a quick look as he turned downhill through a parklike area shaded by pines. Midway down the hill the road bent past a well-kept old house on the left. Corry had a brief glimpse of a sign that said *Ranger*-something-or-other. Just below were several well-restored much older buildings.

Tip smiled. "It's Gastons' Mills," he said triumphantly.

Corry saw the name on a sign as he spoke. She remembered having heard it before, but it meant nothing to her.

"So?"

Tip turned into the parking area. "You don't know? Some of Grandfather's best stories were ones Great-Grandfather told him about camping here one summer in the 1880s. Your grandfather must have told your dad."

"Maybe," Corry said as she got out of the car. "Nobody ever told me."

"They came here the first year of the 'Forest and Stream Hunting and Fishing Club'—a dozen or so 'good fellows' in their twenties, complete with a cook and two helpers," Tip explained as he unloaded the picnic hamper, a canvas bag, and the tarpaulin. "From some of the stories, you would think they were little kids. To hear Grandfather tell it, they seemed to do more lazing around and playing jokes on each other than hunting and fishing."

Carrying the hamper between them, Tip and Corry moved upstream to a grassy spot near the water where the dark pines would not loom too closely over them. The creek was wide and the tree-clad hillside opposite bright with new leaves.

"Who all were they?"

"I'm not sure. Some were connected with the potteries, I think. Owners's sons, some of them. The names wouldn't have meant much to Grandfather."

Corry stretched out her shawl and dipped through the

grass like a dancer, dreamily. Standing with her back to the water's edge, she looked across the grass and narrow road to the pines, intently, as if she were trying to see not through their branches, but the years.

"He might have stood right where I'm standing," she said. "It feels strange. Like a hundred years was no time at all. But it would have been more woodsy. Not so park-ish. The pine trees aren't anywhere near that old. They don't feel right, somehow. . . ."

But hunger and the picnic hamper drew her back.

Beneath the hamper's lid was a polished board that turned out to be the center leaf of a table which unfolded up and outward. With its supports snapped fast to the hamper frame, it made a tiny table for two to match the folding chairs from the canvas bag. Fitted into the compartments that had been concealed under the collapsible table were plates and cups, plastic boxes of sandwiches, pasta salad, fruit salad and spice cake and, surprisingly, cans of iced tea as well as root beer.

"Where'd you get all this? And the weird picnic basket?"

"Mrs. Frowd. And the attic." Tip handed her the forks and napkins. "The initials on the leather label are almost worn off, but they look like LTC. Lucas and Cordelia Tipson, that would be. There are fitted tin boxes, and bottles covered with woven caning that belong in it, but Mrs. Frowd said that even if they were washed, and safe after eighty or ninety years to put food in, they would probably make everything taste like attic floor."

Corry served salad onto two plates and, helping herself

147

to a sandwich, sat down gingerly on one of the spindly-looking chairs.

"Mm, *goo'*," she said around a mouthful of homemade bread, thin-sliced roast beef, and creamy horseradish. "I' fee' safer on the groun', 'ough." The chair squeaked with even the slightest movement.

"No sooner said than done, no sooner wished than won," Tip announced with mock-gallantry, spreading out the tarp and a tablecloth to cover it. "The Hunting and Fishing Club used camp-stools. Grandfather had an old picture of them all lined up on 'em."

"Cooks and campstools. And cots, I bet. Pretty comfy camping," Corry said, and then giggled self-consciously at the alliteration.

"They didn't come just for the all-us-men lark, either," Tip said with a sideways look. "They went serenading up over the hill where there was a pretty farmer's daughter. And they had Ladies' Days. They'd bring out a wagonload or so of sisters and other girls to picnic and play baseball. I expect Cordelia came."

"I didn't know girls played baseball a hundred years ago," Corry said in surprise. "I though they only played ladylike games like badminton or croquet."

Tip moved closer, to refill her glass of iced tea. "Great-Grandfather and Cordelia might even have got engaged here. Maybe they took a walk downstream away from the others, and—"

"I wish I knew more about baseball," Corry said absently, wrinkling her brow. "Do you know anything about the Pirates? Don's taking me to the Pirates' game next

Saturday. He knows their batting averages and lifetime statistics and all that, but I don't even know who's who."

"You don't need to," Tip said quietly after a moment. "Their names are on their uniform shirts." He rose and went to the table for another root beer.

"My dad gets back tomorrow," he announced, keeping his back to her. "You can tell your mother all about me today, if you want. It won't matter. I probably won't be here long."

Corry looked up anxiously. "He won't take you away now, not when school's so near over. Will he?"

Tip shrugged. "It depends what mood he's in. It's not that he really cares *what* I do. So long as it was his idea. At least it hasn't cost him anything. The refund he'll get from good old Litchfield Academy will come to more than I've spent here."

"I still don't see why you want to stay," Corry said slowly. "It used to be, all I dreamed about was getting away. Maybe I don't feel that way—or anyway, not so much— since I found out something about the Tipsons, and learned about the Lotus Ware recipe. But don't you see? There's nothing left of what you're looking for. No Tipson and Sons. No Hunting and Fishing Clubs with cooks. No big-happy-family. It's all gone. You could even say your great-grandmother's 'all gone.' " She looked at him in genuine bafflement. "You could be any place you want. Do any*thing* you want. I don't get it."

She frowned as Tip pulled a small manila envelope from the wicker hamper and held it out to her. "What's this?"

"Open it," Tip said. "I had them make prints for your mother, too."

Corry, pulling out the photographic prints, saw the photo of herself in Cordelia's ivory gown aglow against the attic's shadows, pearls gleaming in the red-gold hair piled high, one hand resting lightly on the slender-legged old table. She looked up, pleased but puzzled.

"That's why," Tip said in his coolest, most amused voice as he helped himself to more pasta salad. "Silly, isn't it?"

The words were light, but when he turned there was no paper bag to hide his meaning.

Twelve

GAIL SHOOK HER head in wonder. "Where's the problem? You really lucked out. *Two* guys! Here—I think these two fit," she added, handing over two more small pieces of the Lotus cup for gluing.

"But what am I supposed to do?" Corry asked anxiously as she sorted through the pieces spread out on the kitchen table. "One minute you think you have a friend and a cousin. The next, you feel like you're being stalked through the woods by strangers."

"More like by puppy dogs," Gail scoffed. "You're only rattled because you didn't hear the patter of their little paws. I *told* you Tip liked you. You just laughed."

"You didn't tell me about Don."

"Well, no," Gail admitted. "I thought he was still one of Angie's puppy dogs. But that only makes it nicer. What

151

you do is enjoy it. You like them both, so go out with them both. Here, reach me that curved piece, will you?"

"But Tip's my *cousin*. I just told you."

"So what? Second cousins aren't illegal. Besides, I only said go out with him, not marry him, for crumbs' sake."

"But—"

"But nothing," Gail said briskly. Then, just as Corry had despaired of making her understand, she reached out hesitantly to cover Corry's hand with her own. "Things change. You can't help it. They just *do*."

Maybe so, Corry thought, but not if she could help it. She wanted a friend and a cousin, not two boyfriends. Not those two, anyway. They were, except for Gail, her only two real friends in the world, and now they wanted to change everything. Make her choose. Well, she wouldn't.

It was easy enough during the week that followed to be busy every out-of-class minute with homework, making a small mold from Liz's detached arm, mixing the slip, and pouring six test castings from the Reggie-and-Liz mold— the extra ones because she had finally caught on that more things could go wrong than she had ever imagined, and also because she had noticed that though the first two had a number of tiny pinholes in the clay, the later castings showed fewer and fewer such imperfections.

The weekend was more difficult. Once the six half-dry "leather-hard" arm castings and sheaves of roses were fastened to the six leather-hard Lizzes, the filigree fixed to the pedestals, and finally the casting marks on the six dried "greenware" figurines sanded and polished away, Sunday afternoon was still left free. Don came over to say that he was painting his mother's kitchen cabinets and needed Corry's steady hand for the trim. Tip phoned to report that he had found a box of old papers and pottery account books and records in the Elysian Way attic, and would she like to come up to help sort through them in hopes of finding family papers? To both invitations Corry had protested that she was too busy. So that it wouldn't be a lie, she turned back to the Lotus cup. Taking its pieces up to the attic, she spread them out as if it were truly a jigsaw puzzle and set to work, this time in earnest.

By suppertime she found that she had actually completed two-thirds of its delicate foot.

The next day was *the* Monday. Her first porcelain firing. Two "greenware" Reggie-and-Lizzes, as unfired pieces were called, rode the bus up to school wrapped in plastic, with a moth-holed wool scarf around that, in Corry's old *Star Wars* lunchbox from middle-school days. The embarrassing lunchbox itself Corry carried in a plastic shoe-shop bag. Turning the figurines over to Mrs. Giorgiadis before homeroom period, Corry felt as if she were giving them up for good. Hurrying to reach her homeroom before the bell she thought, laughing at herself, that it must be a little like sending your kids away to college or out into the world. They were bound to come back different. Better and stronger, you hoped. Not cracked.

Cracked. Awful word. And even if the figures themselves didn't crack, what about the roses and filigree pedestal? If cake-icing filigree could crack away from a framework, clay must be even worse. Maybe *lots* worse. But

Corry found even that suspense and excitement dimmed by the new and painful shyness that had come to spoil as simple a thing as saying "Hi" to Don or Tip in the hall between classes. Art appreciation class was worst of all, with the kiln only yards away beyond the wall and the two boys sitting side by side in the dark behind her as slides of French Impressionist paintings flashed on the wall-screen. Corry hunched over her notebook, doodling starbursts in the dim light, scarcely hearing Mrs. Giorgiadis's remarks or the discussion between one slide and the next.

On Tuesday Corry took her lunch to school, and when third period was over made a dash up the stairs and down the crowded hall to Mrs. Giorgiadis's room. "And there goes Flutie, carrying the ball instead of passing it," Tike Persons boomed in a sports-announcer's twang as she passed him. "He sees an opening. Will he make it? Will—"

"Goodness," Mrs. Giorgiadis said as Corry hurried in and closed the door behind her. "You look as if you'd just done a lap around the track."

"I hurried." Corry dropped her books on the table. "The kiln. Is it cool enough? Have you opened it?"

"Yes, come on back." Mrs. Giorigiadis led the way to the inner door. "But I hate to tell you—it's disappointing. The pyrometer stopped at 2200 degrees. It's supposed to be able to go to 2300, but . . ." She shrugged helplessly. "It may be my fault. I'm not familiar with the kiln yet. And from what I've read so far, even 2300 may not do it. One book says 2265 to 2335 degrees, and another says 2375. So it's all a bit like working in the dark."

The kiln was a top-loading model, and the fire-brick-insulated top had already been removed. The Reggie-and-Liz stood alone on its ceramic "setter" disk, looking startled and palely tragical. A thin but fatal crack divided them, and Liz had dropped her arm as well as her roses.

"Oh, no!" Corry groaned. "They look like Jane Eyre and Mr. Rochester in the scene where the priest says 'Speak now or forever hold your peace,' and old whoosit up and stops the wedding."

Mrs. Giorgiadis laughed. "They do, don't they? But don't worry," she added reassuringly. "We still have the other casting you brought. We may do better with a longer firing-period."

Corry reached into the kiln and brought out figures and setter disk together. "They're stuck." She gave a hard tug. "*Really* stuck." Even more alarming, their surface was marred by a number of tiny black specks.

"Careful." Mrs. Giorgiadis took the Reggie-and-Liz and turned it around, examining it closely. She shook her head. "I put it on a setter because the shelf has drips of glaze on it and I was afraid your figurine might stick, but there must have been a smear of glaze on the setter, too, from an earlier firing. I don't think we can get it off without breaking some of the filigree."

"Why worry? It's spoiled anyhow." Corry scowled at the bridal pair. "I wish I knew for sure why they cracked. Why do people want to become potters at all if things go wrong all the time? Even for potters who know what they're doing."

"Oh, it's not as bad as all that," Mrs. Giorgiadis objected. "The more experienced you are, the more control you have."

Corry looked glum. "A friend of mine, Mr. Hankins, says sometimes half the pieces in a kiln full of Lotus Ware came out broken or spoiled. He knows, too. The father of a friend of his worked at Knowles, Taylor and Knowles back when they made it."

But wasn't one perfect Lotus cup—wasn't that worth a dozen blistered or broken ones? A dozen disappointments?

Mrs. Giorgiadis looked up from rummaging through her top tool drawer for a thin-bladed knife and smiled to see Corry's thoughtful expression. "You're thinking it was worth it, aren't you? What's too bad is that they tried to sell Lotus through their regular outlets as if it were just another product line. In more exclusive shops at higher prices—like Wedgewood or Belleek—it might still be selling. Ah, here we go."

She slid the corner of a putty knife under the filigreed pedestal and worked it toward the spot where the rim was stuck fast. With a little *snap!* the bridal pair popped loose, leaving a sliver of its base still on the setter.

"It doesn't matter." Corry looked at the broken edge and then held the Reggie-and-Liz up to the light. "You're right. It didn't get fired enough. It's so brittle. And it isn't—what's the word for 'glassified?'"

"Vitrified."

"That's it," Corry said. "It ought to be see-through-able."

Mrs. Giorgiadis laughed. "'Translucent.' Well, we'll

156

try again tomorrow. I'll come in early so we can do a longer, slower firing."

That evening when the supper dishes had been washed and dried, Mrs. Tipson mixed a batch of royal icing for a wedding cake ordered for Saturday and soon was deftly piping out pale pink roses. Corry in her preoccupation did not notice her mother's watchful frown as she raced through her homework—even the problems with three equations with three variables—and at eight-thirty bundled her books back into the bookbag.

Up in the stillness of the attic workroom, Corry sat staring accusingly at the four remaining greenware Reggie-and-Lizzes. Would they *all* come out in tiny black zits? The sight of the speckled and split-up Reggie and Liz hadn't really bothered her in the way she had expected. Not even after all that work. It wasn't that she had gone off weddings. Or cakes. For decorating or eating at least. Perhaps— perhaps while she still thought she might get to train as a pastry cook and one day open *April's Cakes*, the Reggie-and-Lizzes had been a way of making those tomorrows seem more real. Now they felt more like guinea pigs in an experiment. What *had* gone wrong? With a new objectivity, she saw that if they really turned out anything like Lotus, their snowy elegance might look great on her mother's most expensive wedding cakes, but—on a little seventy-five or hundred-dollar one with daisy borders or pink roses? They would look like royalty at a square dance. Yet the idea of designing a "second string" pair. . . . No. She would make a dozen or so—a two- or three-year supply, and for the less

157

expensive cakes, they would make do for now with the old-style Dick-and-Janes. For the independent study project proposal she would have to think up another design. Something really good. Something all her own.

While her mind wandered in search of ideas, her fingers moved among the Lotus chips, sorting out a shallow curve here, a bit of rim there. Perhaps it was because her concentration was open, unfocused as she looked over the bone-white shards and slivers, but when she pushed her chair back at last, the cup's foot stood on its own rim. Splinters were missing, and in one spot a small triangle gaped in the rippled seashell-surface, but it was real progress. What she really ought to do, she thought, was finish the repairs and give it back to Tip. For an apology. A peace offering. She hated not talking to him. Ducking around corners. Not knowing what to say to him. Tomorrow, she promised herself. Tomorrow she would just walk up to him and say—something. As if nothing had happened at all. Just thinking about it was a relief.

She would have felt even better if there hadn't been Saturday and Don to worry about.

If the first school-kiln firing had been disappointing, so was the second. When, in the minute or two before the fifth-period bell the door was lifted after the cool-down, the beautiful filigree which had not been visible through the peephole was gone, cracked into bits and scattered around the kiln as if it had been popped like popcorn.

"And more black specks. Great. Just great," Corry said despairingly. "It's *never* going to work."

"Don't *say* that!" Mrs. Giorgiadis exclaimed. "You've got me hooked now. And you've learned enough to write a realistic project description for your course application. We'll find out what went wrong. . . . Oops, there's the bell. Leave the poor things there for now."

Corry's disappointment was so sharp that both art and anatomy class slid past almost unnoticed. The "poor things" rode home jammed into her bookbag. To make the day complete, as she alighted from the bus, the bookbag took a smart crack against the folding door when Don, close behind, stumbled on the top step and almost fell.

Corry yelped indignantly. "Hey!" But when she turned and discovered it had been Don, her indignation faded.

"What's the matter? You look like a—a cold tapioca pudding." She resisted the temptation to check her bookbag to see what was making the faint clinking sound. Why worry? The Reggie-and-Liz was already ruined.

Don grinned weakly. "Pale and clammy? That's me. Maybe you better keep clear. I must be coming down with the flu or something."

Corry felt a guilty rush of relief. No baseball game or dinner out? No coming home late and saying goodnight on the porch and getting kissed on target?

Even as the thought shaped itself her cheeks reddened, and she said quickly, "Maybe if you go to bed right away and stay home tomorrow, it'll be gone by Saturday. And drink lots of juice," she added awkwardly.

She wasn't used to feeling awkward with Don. She hated it. And him for causing it. Or at least she would have if he didn't look so much like a big, lolloping puppy (*why*

159

did Gail have to mention puppies?) about to be sick on the sidewalk.

"Here, I'll carry your books," she said hastily.

Corry found her mother in the attic bathroom wrestling with the S-trap under the sink. A new S-trap lay on the floor. "What a way to spend a day off!" April Tipson exclaimed. She sat back on her heels and wiped her forehead with her arm. "I been wrestling with this blasted joint for half an hour at least. And I've still got the vacuuming to do. You turn on the spigot and the fool pipe joint leaks like a colander, but oh, turn off the water and try to disconnect the blamed thing, and will it budge? Not a twitch."

She gave the pipe a loud whack with the wrench and stood up. "I guess I'll have to ask Ben Chappick to have a go at it after all. Actually, I been thinking—if we got it fixed, and made a start at clearing out the back rooms and painting up, then after you've finished your Reggie-and-Lizzes we'll have us a little apartment to rent. There'd have to be some kind of kitchenette, though. That's a problem."

Corry looked at the heaped-up cartons standing by the stairwell. "What are you going to do with that stuff?" It looked to be mostly junk—chipped dishes, faded curtains, the battered muffin tin, and more.

"Throw it out. Why? You want to go through it?"

"No, no," Corry said hastily. "It's just—you *never* throw stuff out."

"Well, now I do." Mrs. Tipson picked up one carton. "Supper's early. Five-thirty, so I can finish baking the cakes."

When she had gone, Corry unrolled the newspaper in

160

which she had wrapped the figurine and stared glumly at the wreckage. The knock against the bus door had sheared off the pedestal and a wide swatch of Liz's skirt. Picking up the piece of skirt, Corry looked at the broken edge, and then held the shard up to the light. It still looked more like ordinary china than anything, neither glassy along the break nor translucent. But it was more brittle than china would be.

Voices floated up from below, but Corry only half heard, and she was startled when Mr. Hankins knocked on the stairwell wall. She was glad to see him, and fascinated when he pointed out the slight difference in the smoothness and density along the broken edges between the first cracked figurine and the second.

"You see the difference that hundred degrees made? The closer you come to the right temperature for Mr. Poole's formula, the faster the change. As for the cracking, it could be from too many pinholes or too fast a firing or cool-down, or even all three." About the black specks he had no idea at all.

Black specks or no, Corry was elated as she headed downstairs to supper, but it was a new feeling, not the eager impatience of the weeks past. It didn't matter about the Reggie-and-Lizzes being ruined. Seeing results of the first chemical changes from molecules of clay and feldspar to slick-sided glassy ones was fascinating. Maybe taking chemistry next year wouldn't be as grisly as she feared. Once you knew—

April Tipson stood at the table in the front hall, her hand on the telephone. She looked up as Corry appeared on the landing above.

"It's Don," she said. "He's in the hospital. I called to ask Ben about the attic sink, and Dickie answered. He says their folks took Don over to Emergency about fifteen minutes ago."

It was a kidney infection, a disappointingly (from Don's point of view), unglamorous but alarmingly dramatic ailment until the antibiotics began to take effect. By Saturday afternoon the worst was over. Mr. Chappick and Dickie ended up going to the Pirates game. Corry and Don watched it on the TV set in Don's hospital room.

The alternation between high fever and bone-shaking chills had left Don weak and almost as white as his sheets. And short-tempered. The bed needed adjusting. His I.V. needle itched fiercely and had to be changed to his other arm. Whosis tried to steal second base when any idiot could see that the second baseman, who had eyes in the back of his head, was praying for a chance to pick him off. The sound was too loud. Or too low. He didn't want orange juice. Wasn't there any apple juice?

"Yish!" Corry exclaimed as the eighth inning finished at last. "They'll be glad to see *you* roll out the front door."

"Why don't you roll away yourself," Don said fretfully. "You want to. You could be out whizzing around with Tip Meredith. Doing something 'interesting.' You nearly fell asleep while Pena was up at bat. You're probably glad you didn't have to go all the way up to Pittsburgh to be bored."

Corry sat up straight, as startled and hurt as if the

162

proverbial friendly puppy had up and bitten her, for no reason at all. At least—he couldn't have *known* she was glad. . . .

"Oh, don't go staring at me like a stuffed squirrel." Don leaned back against the pillows. He sounded less snappish, but still grumpy. "I didn't think you'd play Angie's kind of games."

Corry was bewildered. "Games?"

Don kept one eye on the TV, watching for the end of the commercials. "Oh, come on. Pretending you like something you couldn't care less about? Like baseball. And how about 'On-Again-Off-Again?' Glad to see me one day, and acting like I had the purple pimple plague the next. What's that? 'Keep-'em-Guessing?' "

"But I haven't been," Corry protested. "I just—"

"What else would you call sticking your head in your locker and pretending you don't see me? Or ducking into the library when you see me coming?" He held up a warning hand. "Forget it. Pena's coming up to bat again."

He watched for a while with an unfamiliar, mulish look, and then fell asleep halfway through the inning. Corry turned the sound down and left, closing the door behind her. Riding down alone in the elevator, she stretched up her arms and with a dramatic groan demanded, "What *else* can go wrong?"

The doors opened wide as she spoke, and at the next floor down a gray-haired doctor with a youngish face got in. He nodded gravely at her with a humorous glint in his eye.

"Almost anything," he said.

Thirteen

"YOUR COUSIN!" April Tipson shook her head again, as if the idea still would not fit in. "And he's been living up in that big house all alone? It sounds pretty weird, if you ask me. His mom and *dad* sound pretty weird. It's too bad. He seems like a nice kid, only he's got such good manners you can't be sure. And here I thought he was sweet on you."

She trailed off into thoughtfulness and Corry, seeing her vague look of disappointment, guessed that she had been baking her own pie in the sky—a wedding, a handsome house, being able to afford a car? And nice clothes. Corry saw in her own imagination the peach and green sweater in Ogilvies' department store window. Thirty-nine ninety-five. She pushed the thought away.

"I think he is," she said abruptly. "Gail says so, anyhow, and on our picnic Saturday he was kind of—I don't know. Happy-miserable. Like Bingo is when he wants a

big hug but's afraid he might get a kick in the slats instead."
Bingo was the big Labrador next door, and with Mr. Notts
for an owner, he had good reason to be concerned for his
slats. Corry grinned in spite of herself. "Gail called Tip and
Don 'puppy dogs,' and now I can't stop."

"About Tip, you might be righter'n you think," Mrs.
Tipson observed. "It sounds like his folks've pretty much
kicked him back and forth. A quiet kid like him, getting
himself bumped out of all those schools? I can believe he
did it just to get sent home, but then all they did was boot
him off to another one."

"And now me, too," Corry said unhappily. "But I don't
feel about him like he wants me to. And I'm not who he
wants me to *be*. I think he wants me to play Great-Grandma
Cordelia. He wants . . ."

For a moment it seemed sadly, piercingly clear. He
dreamed of the past as she had dreamed of the future—as
a refuge. But it was that and more. It was as if he wanted
to make himself an island outside of the present. To rein-
vent the Tipsons and regain something of all that he—that
they—had lost. A place and people to belong to. Slower
days. Uncomplicated pleasures. Paradise on Elysian Way.
Not much to ask!

The Elysian Fields. . . .

Who knows? Maybe the name of the street put the
idea of coming here into his head in the first place.

But the past hadn't been all *that* great. It couldn't have
been. The young Cordelia of the photo-mural in the museum
didn't look like she lived in paradise. Even if later she and
Lucas Henry had a sort of Eden of their own, there had been

a snake in it somewhere, because the rest of the Tipsons sure
got driven out.

"What am I supposed to do?" she asked miserably.
Avoiding Tip and Don hadn't meant avoiding uncomfortable situations. It had only made everything worse. "Don
said I was playing games, like Angie Dalla. But that's unfair. I *wasn't*. It's just I didn't know how to explain."

Her mother squinted as she rethreaded her needle.
"Seems to me you don't give them two credit for maybe
having feelings as touchy as yours are. My guess is, all Don's
peck on the cheek and asking you out on a real date means
is something like 'Hey, I just noticed you're not my sister.'
Then you start ducking around corners, what's he supposed
to think? It sure as apples doesn't tell him, 'I like it fine
being your sister, *period*.' "

"You mean say *that*? Right out?" Corry faltered.

"If that's what you mean. Why not? You want to shut
a door on something, shut it. You want to leave it open a
crack, say 'Right now I like it fine the way things are,
OK?' " Mrs. Tipson shook her head. "Trouble with you,
Corry Tipson, is you're too much like your dad."

Corry grew still. *How?* she wanted desperately to ask,
but when it came to her father, questions as often as not
drove her mother into an unhappy silence.

The torn sheet lay forgotten in Mrs. Tipson's lap. "He
never had a mean thought in his head, your dad," she said
slowly, "but he was always getting himself in hot water
because he went at things so round-about, always second-
guessing. He'd go off with the grocery list and see mayonnaise on it and think, 'April uses French dressing on lettuce

and *hates* mayonnaise on sandwiches, so she's got to be getting it for me. But she loves mustard. I'll get mustard instead. She'll like that.' So then I'd be teed off because the mayo was to go in the tuna casserole for supper. Every job he had, he'd try to please the boss at work that way—second-guessing him. He'd always do it once too often and get himself fired."

"You didn't fire him," Corry ventured.

Mrs. Tipson smiled. "Gosh, no. When I wasn't teed off, I loved him for it. I mean, he really *cared*. That year he taught school—"

Corry blinked. She hadn't known her father had taught school.

Her mother saw her surprise and nodded. "Yeah, after he got out of the army. English. Spring semester my senior year. But he was only substituting. Anyhow, there he is: Teaching senior English, he's supposed to teach the stuff in the book, right? But the principal tells him how low our reading scores'd been on some big test or other, so Luke wants to please him, maybe make a good enough impression to get a full-time job if one turns up. What he does is start assigning extra work, dittoing off extra stories and poems, firing us up. Lots of the class did real good on the next couple tests, but it wasn't a pat on the head he got. I disremember what most of the stories were, but there was this one by—what's his name? Hemingway?—by Hemingway that had this Indian woman having a baby in it. Maybe it was that or one of the other stories, but somebody's folks got shocked and made a big prune-faced stink. Next thing we knew, we had a new substitute."

Corry stared at her mother in astonishment. "Daddy was *your* teacher? You didn't even like English."

Her mother grinned. "That didn't keep me from liking him. He had this shy smile, like you got, that made my knees feel like Jell-O."

Corry was fascinated. "But if he was so shy and 'round-about' how'd he ever get up nerve to propose?"

Mrs. Tipson laughed ruefully. "He never did. When he showed up at our graduation, I just up and told him he was the nicest man I'd ever met. He got real flustered because he liked *me* such a lot—I was real pretty back then, would you believe it?—but he was sure I'd never love him back. He decided what I really meant was, since I'd almost flunked English and didn't have a job lined up, I just wanted somebody to tutor me. It was July before I got him convinced my mind wasn't on grammar. He—" She broke off abruptly and fished in her pocket for a tissue. As she blew her nose, Corry saw the tears gleaming through her lashes.

"So I told him I wished he'd ask, so I could say yes. And he did, and I did." She looked around for her needle and began to stitch away busily as if the subject were closed.

Corry leaned forward, hugging her knees, and tried to remember the gentle, unsure man who had been her father. Lucas Henry Tipson II. But all that she could conjure up was a reassuring shadow in her bedroom doorway, the echo of old arguments, and the memory of her mother in her bathrobe, huddled in the dark front hall on the bottom stair-step, watching, watching the door.

"About the attic," Mrs. Tipson said abruptly. "How soon'll you be finished casting those new Dick-and-Janes?"

168

"Reggie-and-Lizzes," Corry said automatically. "Why?"

"I've been thinking, the sooner we get the attic fixed up, the sooner we'll be getting that hundred and fifty a month for it."

"But—next year!" Corry protested in dismay. "My individual study project. Can't it wait until after that? Where'll I work?"

"I've been thinking about that, too," her mother said. "Once you've learned how and made the cake figures, you *know* how. And if you're that good, you don't need to waste half a semester's credit on it when you could be taking typing."

Corry, in her distress, could not find her tongue. A dozen objections welled up confusedly, but what would her mother care for any of them? The attic had been nothing but a catch-all for how long? Fifty years. She had understood it to be hers for as long as the project took. Not that her mother had said so, but— The wallpaper might be peeling, and the windows and woodwork still grimy, but it had begun to feel and look a bit like a real potter's studio.

"Cat got your tongue? I asked how soon before you're finished."

"I d-don't know." It was the truth, but Corry could only stammer out the words. "I have to get the f-firing right first. And m-make enough more clay for all the Reggie-and-Lizzes."

Her mother nodded. "OK, say the end of June. Then even if you get a summer job, there'll be time for us to pitch in and fix the attic up real nice by September. Next week you can lend a hand clearing out the little room next to the bathroom, so when Ben comes over to look at that sink trap, he can give me an idea how much he'd charge to plumb us a kitchen in there. And do the wiring. He rewired his own house, and he'd be cheaper'n an electrician. And I oughta be able to pick up a used stove and fridge pretty cheap."

She had it all planned out. Corry fought to keep back the tears.

"But tomorrow I was going to write my project proposal. You have to sign the application. I'm going to make a—a p-porcelain cake," Corry lied desperately, the idea unfolding miraculously into truth as she spoke. "It'll have s-sixteen separate slices that fit together into a cake, and it'll be funny and beautiful at the same time. With white roses and lacework a-and a place in the middle for a Reggie-and-Liz to stand. You never want to put up a sign in the front window, but why not a china cake?"

As she spoke, she knew that she really meant to do it. Wanted desperately to do it: make it beautiful and funny at the same time. . . . She rose and crossed to the table by the window to take away the glass bowl of fake fruit that stood there, then turned to watch her mother anxiously.

Mrs. Tipson looked thoughtfully at the empty space, but only for a moment or two.

"It's a nice idea, OK," she granted. "But the year's rent'll be well over a thousand dollars toward your college money. Besides, this pottery stuff takes too much of your time. You've been cutting back on pretty near everything else. I didn't mind doing that last cake all by myself. That's

OK. It's worth it the way that Reggie-and-Liz turned out. But you've been short-changing your homework, too, reading that pottery book instead and thinking I don't notice. So the study project's out, and that's flat."

Up in the attic after supper, Corry put her head down among the fragments of the Lotus cup and cried tears more of frustration than of grief. It was awful being so shy with your own mother that you couldn't put up a good fight for something you cared about. All the really good arguments dawned on you half an hour after it was all over. Most unfair of all, her mother's arguments were always right at hand, and she wasn't shy about letting fly with them. *And that's flat.*

If only, Corry thought in despair, she hadn't done such an enthusiastic cleanup job, her mother would never have seen the attic's possibilities. It would have been enough to clear a space for the tables, and a path to them. Stupid!

It was too much. First the veto of her Harlan Institute plans, even though that had not been as hard to take as she had expected. Now, two far deeper disappointments. For they *were* deeper. If the studio were hers to keep, she could have given up the individual study project with no more than a passing regret. She would have gone on with the work itself, school credit or no.

And still could.

Still *would*.

But not just a witty china cake. . . .

She turned over and over in her fingers a section of

the mock coral from the cup's slender, intricate stem. Four stems, really. Branching stems of Lotus coral twined together at this one point. . . .

Impossible to make a cast of it.

But of the foot? And the cup's bowl? Make molds from them, and the castings would shrink as they dried, making the copy smaller than the cup itself. But still lovely.

And if she could learn to pipe the delicate, knobbly strands of coral, joining them together as soon as they had dried enough to handle? And joining foot to stem to fluted bowl?

Corry shivered. It would never work. But if it did. . . . If it did, she would work in the cellar. In the shed out back. Wherever. And if not doing an official school project meant the school kiln was out, then—then there would be another kiln somewhere. She dried here eyes on her shirttail and began sorting out bits of stem.

Slowly, painstakingly, with a new intensity of concentration, Corry worked to fit one fragment to another, and those two to yet another. When her progress on the stem faltered, she returned to the fluted shell-like cup, abandoning it in turn to fit a splinter to the almost-completed foot. Some matchings came with systematic comparison, others in flashes of insight. She grew thirsty, but could not bear to stop even long enough to go downstairs for a drink of water. After a while so few pieces were left unmatched that it was impossible to stop, even though her watch told her that it was past midnight.

When the last fragment had been cemented into the cup's rim, Corry held the three parts, foot, stem and cup, together, and drew in her breath in wonder. The white, translucent cup with its missing bits and spiderweb of seams was perhaps no more than a ghost of its long-ago self, but its loveliness was like a ripple of music caught and held.

When she reached her own room, Corry managed to kick off her shoes, but fell into bed still clothed and was asleep even as she burrowed into her pillow.

In the hospital lounge area by the elevators, Corry sat down to tape a sheet of drawing-paper to hang like a flag from the crooked stick she had broken from the old sycamore in front of the Tipson house. She might not be able to "be direct," as her mother advised, but she had to try, at least, to mend things with Don. Make him laugh, anyhow.

At the "Come in" that answered her tap on the door, Corry stuck her white flag out past the doorframe. For a moment there was only silence in the room beyond. Then she heard Don's guffaw. "Corry?"

She stuck her head around the door. "All clear?"

"Yeah, all clear," Don agreed, but gave a nod toward the room's other bed, where a middle-aged man lay propped up, watching a golf tournament on the TV.

Don reached out a hand toward the truce flag as Corry crossed to the bedroom chair. "Let's see that."

On its face was a lively comic drawing of a pig-tailed, saucer-eyed child peering around a door, holding a truce flag—and on her flag was drawn a second child and *her* flag, on which could be seen yet another. And another, on and on as far as Corry's pen could manage the finer and finer detail.

"It's great," he said with a grin. "You really used to look like that. Ready to hop off and away if anybody even sneezed."

"I still feel like that lots," she said, keeping her eyes on the fifteenth green at the Atlanta Country Club. "Almost all the time."

Don was silent for a moment, digesting that, and Corry imagined she could almost hear the wheels turning in his mind. Even so, her mother was right about one thing. Don might be her best friend—beside Gail—yet she had no idea what really went on in his head, even though sometimes it seemed he saw straight into hers. She had never asked. Or even thought about it much until now.

"Well, I like it," he said abruptly. "Lots. Can I keep it?"

Corry felt herself flush with relief and pleasure. It *felt* as if he had understood. With an effort, she met his gaze. "Sure. It's yours. How do you feel? You look lots better."

"I feel lots better. I'm tired, but no more chills. How's the potting going?"

Corry rolled her eyes toward the ceiling. "Awful. And great," she said. She explained about the failed firing, Mr. Hankins's latest visit and advice, and the axe her mother had dropped on the school study project.

"But you're going ahead anyhow?"

Corry wasn't sure whether the quirk she heard in his voice meant that he was surprised or impressed or thought she was missing a major marble.

"I've got to." She shrugged helplessly, and groped for the right words. "If I don't, it'd be like I—like I abandoned

174

ship. But I wish I had a job Saturdays. I'll need to make more clay pretty soon, and I maybe'll have to pay for the ingredients I don't have enough of. Money. Your dad doesn't need a plumber's assistant this summer, does he?"

Don grinned. "He's got me. How much have you got left in your birthday account?"

"Seven-fifty."

"Well, if you scrape bottom, I saved a lot more than seven-fifty by missing dinner up in Pittsburgh," he said with a casual, sideways look. "And your friend Meredith's folks must keep the stuff around the house by the trashbag-full."

"Oh, sure. Anyway, he's my cousin, not my friend. At least," she added quickly, "not 'friend' with quotation marks, the way you mean it."

"Your *cousin?*" Don stared.

Corry lifted her chin. "But I wouldn't borrow from either of you. It's got to be my project. I want it to be something *I* do. All on my own."

Don shook his head as if to clear it, and dropped back against his pillows. "Cousin!" he muttered, and then drummed on the mattress in comic exasperation. "For Pete's sake, Corry! If you bail out or put the potting on hold because you don't want to borrow a couple crummy dollars, you've got Mexican refried beans for brains. 'All on your own?' Since when? With school electricity? Free stuff from everybody and his uncle? Getting your frit fired and milled for free? What's different about money, except it's more— impersonal? And you can pay it back, for crumb's sake."

Corry hesitated. It was all true. And she wanted very much to keep going. "I guess you're right," she said at last.

175

But her mother's rule of *Never be beholden* had been drummed into her for so long that breaking it would not be easy.

Don's outburst had tired him, and his answering grin seemed paler. "Well, my wallet's at home, so don't go broke till I get out of here. And keep your fingers crossed. The doctor says with any luck I can go home tomorrow."

As he spoke, a hesitant knock came at the door, and they turned to see old Mr. Hankins in his neat, shabby Sunday suit.

"Good afternoon, Cordelia. And young Chappick. Did I hear you say you may be freed tomorrow? My congratulations."

Mr. Hankins had made a detour on his daily walk to check on Don's progress, and when he left, Corry went with him. They reached the main entrance on Fifth Street in the middle of Corry's hesitant explanation of the process by which she hoped to reproduce the Lotus cup, and Mr. Hankins stopped short.

"But I thought that was always in your mind."

"No-o." Embarrassed, Corry looked at the scuffed toes of her white shoes. She *had* let him think so. "Not really. Anyhow, if I'd tried it early on, I'd've given up a month ago."

"Ah!" Mr. Hankins smiled. "But now you've learned the artist-potter's lesson—that failure is the key to learning."

Corry looked up at him shyly, and laughed. "Yeah. It would be neat if that worked with algebra too."

The old man, seeing she had something more on her mind, tilted his head questioningly. "Yes?"

176

"It's just—everybody's been so nice. They *give* me stuff, when I never asked them to. Even when I asked such dumb questions they had to know I wasn't sure which end was up. Why? Mom's always going on about how unfriendly a town it is, but—"

Mr. Hankins tucked her hand under his arm. "Come. I don't like to be away from Mrs. Hankins for too long, so you'll have to join me on my walk. As for people here, I would say your mother is both right and wrong. I believe she still misses her old, very close-knit neighborhood in Pittsburgh, and perhaps we do come out on the short end of that comparison. City folk seem to expect all small towns to be—cosier." At the corner by the synagogue, he turned up toward Sixth Street.

"But why—"

"The *work*, my dear. Most of the potteries may be gone, but however dwindled, this is still a pottery town." He smiled down at her. "There is a very great pleasure in finding a young person interested in your craft, your industry, for something other than just 'a job.' On fire to learn. Eager to work. If you succeed in producing something like the old Lotus Ware, they'll feel they had a part in it. And *that* is a great pleasure. As for your worries about the school kiln, Ralph Ginger tells me that it very likely won't do anyway. You'll need to fire to at least 2350 degrees. He tells me the Ferro porcelain plant up in the East End fires in that range. You might find them glad to help too. But tell me more about the cup. Have you thought how you will fill in the holes so that you can make the mold?"

Mr. Hankins, despite his old-fashioned formality, was

easier to talk to than anyone Corry could think of. He was interested and attentive and, most of all, encouraging. The news of Mrs. Tipson's proposed attic apartment distressed him.

"But where will you work?"

"The cellar, maybe, if I can get it clean enough," Corry said.

"But the coal dust!"

"As soon as the furnace is off for the summer and the coal bin shut up, it should be OK," Corry sounded more cheerful about it than she felt.

Reaching the corner of Sixth and Jackson, Mr. Hankins wavered for a moment, and then crossed the street, heading toward Seventh instead of Fourth. "I must show you where my old friend Albert set up our little pottery studio," he said. "The equipment will have been sold years ago, after Albert died and I gave up decorating, but the studio would be just the place for you if young Brian, Albert's boy, hadn't sold the house. I saw the sign was down last week."

The "pottery studio" turned out to be an old frame garage behind a handsome but sadly shabby Victorian house. The house was still vacant, its windows curtainless. The garage leaned sideways at an angle that would have been even more alarming if it had not had two stout maple trees to lean against. The two small windows were thick with grime, and the clapboarding looked as if it had not been painted since the 1930s.

Mr. Hankins chuckled. "No need to be polite. But it's not as ramshackle as it looks. Albert reinforced the frame from inside." Drawing the handkerchief from his suit pocket, he reached out to wipe the nearest dirty window pane.

"Oh! Don't use your good hankie. Here, I've got a couple of tissues." Corry reached for her pocket.

Because the windows, one on each side of the garage, admitted so little light, there was not much to be seen through the small circle she cleared in the grime. Only a dark, humped shape that might have been a car.

Mr. Hankins gave the bottom window sash a tentative push.

"Hah! It never did fasten properly," he said with satisfaction, pushing it up until it stuck.

Corry looked around anxiously. "Do you think you really ought to—"

"I have no intention of breaking in, my dear." He reached inside and felt along the wall. "Ah, here we are: the light switch."

Inside, a light flickered on under a metal shade. In the moment before it sputtered and burnt out, Corry saw that most of the space was taken by an old car, cobwebbed and blanketed in dust. But directly beneath the window stood a potter's wheel. And in the near corner stood a large, front-loading kiln.

Fourteen

CORRY SPENT ALL day Monday on tenterhooks. Mr. Hankins had promised to ask "young Brian" McCloskey whether the kiln and potter's wheel had been sold with the house. Every time she thought about that, Corry crossed her fingers so hard that it hurt, and much of the rest of the time she chafed because she hadn't been able to find Tip to tell him about the cup. And she hoped—she was sure he would be pleased with her plan to make a copy of it. Only one. For him. He would have to come down for a look. It was too delicate to go traveling around in a lunch box.

Maybe she could ask him for dinner. Things had been uncomfortable for too long. She had to make them all right again, and dinner was a good idea. Make something interesting, like tacos. Her mother liked tacos. Or lasagne. She would ask her mother whether it would be OK.

But Tip was nowhere to be seen. He was in different

180

classes the first three periods, but she usually—when she wasn't trying not to—saw him in the hall on her way from French to English. From the cafeteria line at lunchtime she craned to see the line behind and, when the cashier handed her her change, took her tray on a detour around the tables to make sure he wasn't there. He wasn't. And then she had to hurry, wolfing down her meatball sandwich, so that there would be time to talk to Mrs. Giorgiadis before fourth period.

Mrs. Giorgiadis was eating lunch at her desk. At Corry's news about the study project she was dismayed—almost angry, Corry saw with surprise—and then clearly pleased to hear that Corry not only meant to go on working on her own, but had come up with two new projects.

"I like the idea of a cake made up of slices, too," she said as she handed back the photograph of the cup in the painting. "But I'm not sure I know what you mean by 'elegant and funny.' When you have some sketches, I'd like to see them."

Corry nodded. "The trouble is, I won't have enough clay. And if I keep ruining pieces, I'm not going to have any wedding-cake figures for my mom, either."

Mrs. Giorgiadis went to the sink to rinse out the cup to her thermos. "I took a couple of pottery books home from the library over the weekend to jog my memory, and they reminded me of an answer to just that problem. You really shouldn't be wasting your bridal pairs on test firings. Make something small and simple—a curved tile, or a small cast cup or bowl—to use until you hit the right firing time and temperature." She screwed the cup back onto the thermos. "You'll save clay, the disappointments won't be so traumatic, and you can use the successful test pieces for your glaze tests, too."

Corry made a face. "I know. I read that somewhere too. But I guess I couldn't wait to see the real thing. And I thought when I *did* need more clay, I'd have something good to show everybody who gave me the ingredients. So they'd know I wasn't just making mud pies."

"Take the test tiles to show them. Much more professional. But what are you going to use for a kiln? This one doesn't seem to have enough oomph for your 'old formula' —and we have less than five weeks until school's out."

"There's this old one I know about that nobody's using," Corry said vaguely. She shied away from saying more, for the more you talked about something you wanted fiercely, the worse it was when—*if* you didn't get it. "But I was remembering—the man at Potters' Supply said they fire their saggers at 2350 degrees Fahrenheit. D'you suppose . . ." Mr. Hankins had suggested the Ferro industrial porcelain plant, but she knew no one there.

Mrs. Giorgiadis looked up from packing the thermos and a sandwich box into her canvas carryall.

"That their firing might be right for your clay? That *would* be a piece of luck! You'll have to ask them. A tile or two would take so little room that I'm sure they'd say yes."

"They wouldn't think I was—imposing?" Corry asked uncertainly. "Imposing" was one of her mother's pet frets. She never seemed to think it an imposition to be asked at the last minute to bake an extra cake or two for a bake sale, or to do the Cancer Society collecting for Mrs. Bedell when she was out of town. You did favors. You never asked for them.

Mrs. Giorgiadis looked at her quizzically. "Good gravy, why should they? It won't cost them anything. There's only the one of you. And they may be—probably *are* curious enough about your project to enjoy helping it along. Ask. They won't eat you up."

Corry blushed, but Mrs. Giorgiadis, looking first at her watch and then at the clock, did not notice. It was almost time for the fourth period bell. "Rats! Listen, Corry—I've wanted to ask you: Have you ever thought you might be interested in studying art? There are art schools with excellent ceramics programs, and colleges and universities with strong programs on the art as well as the technical side."

Corry felt a pang of excitement, bitter-sharp. She had known that art schools existed in places like New York or Philadelphia. And one in Pittsburgh even advertised on television. But it had never occurred to her that such a place could have anything to do with everyday life. Not hers, certainly. "Art school." It had almost a ring of the Emerald City to it.

"No," she said regretfully, and said what she knew her mother would say. "It'd be about as practical as taking courses in blowing up balloons."

Tip was not in art appreciation class fifth period. Or in anatomy and physiology. For the first time in weeks Corry felt the old tightness in her stomach. His father must have ordered him home. Or sent someone for him, to be sure he came. He would never see the cup, now. She might never see *him*. . . .

But he would have telephoned, told her somehow, wouldn't he? He might just, with his shy, touchy pride, be avoiding her. Turnabout. Tit for tat.

"For Pete's sake!" Gail exclaimed on the bus ride home when Corry confessed her concern. "And he might've gone home with a headache. Or a toothache. I hate to tell you this, fraught with drama as your life has of late become, but he might even have stayed home with the sniffles."

If the vision of Tip reading in bed with a box of tissues at his elbow was not exactly convincing, it did make Corry smile. And allowed other problems to crowd in upon her. When she went to pick up the extra feldspar she had ordered from Mason Color and Chemical, she would have to ask for alumina, too, to paint on setters so that glazed pieces wouldn't stick. She had forgotten that. *And* she had to ask at the Potters' Supply about having test tiles fired.

Corry arrived home from school in such a rush to leave her books, snatch up a plastic shopping bag, and hurry down to the Potters' Supply that she missed seeing the neatly folded note atop two books on the hall table. On her return with three pounds of feldspar and one of calcined alumina in her bag, she saw the folded square of tablet paper with the neat *Cordelia* in Mr. Hankins's beautiful old-fashioned script. She dropped the bag to snatch it up and read it.

Come up when you can. News!

The news was better than Corry had dared to hope. "Young Brian" McCloskey had told Mr. Hankins that he

184

had a buyer for the old car, but not for the potting equipment. Neither the potter's wheel nor the kiln were in working order, but both should be repairable. If Mr. Hankins wanted them, or any of the other equipment, they were his. As for the house and garage being sold, that was true enough. But it had begun more and more to look as if the buyer was not going to be able to get a mortgage and might have to withdraw his offer. If that happened, Mr. Hankins's young friend would be welcome to use the garage studio until the property did sell. That could take months. A year. The former tenants had left the house in such bad shape that not many prospective buyers took a second look.

Corry forgot Tip as the excitement over the news carried her through dinner and her homework in a rush of energy. "You look awful cheerful for that to be algebra," her mother said suspiciously when she came back to the kitchen for coffee during the commercial break of one of her TV shows. It was not only algebra, but volunteer algebra, so to speak, for Mr. Harmill had given no homework assignment. She finished before 8:30, and spent half an hour sketching the china cake-to-be before going up to repair the last small holes in the Lotus cup.

Her concern about Tip returned as she worked on the cup. With so few weeks to go before summer vacation, how could his father ship him off to a new school? Unless . . . unless he sent him back to Litchfield. But if Mr. Thurwood, the headmaster, was as pickle-tempered and cherrystone-hearted as Tip described him, he probably wouldn't *take* him back.

She felt even less comfortable with the thought that

he might have shut himself up in the big, empty house on Elysian Way. As little as she knew him, she sensed that—unlike Don—if he were hurt, he would turn that hurt inward, upon himself. If he felt as if his parents had abandoned him, and then *she* turned him away . . . Corry's stomach tightened. She bit her lip and wished she hadn't eaten a second helping of creamed chicken and noodles. And what were the family papers he had wanted her help with? He might have been using them as an excuse to see her, but she *had* wanted to know, wanted to sift through them—wanted to learn more about the Tipson potteries, about the Lotus cup itself. And she had said no, that she was going to be busy. Flatly, hurriedly. . . .

As soon as she stepped off the bus Tuesday morning—and without giving herself time for second thoughts—Corry hurried to Tip's homeroom. He was not among the students at the lockers there or settling down in the classroom. Red-cheeked, she slipped in and half-whispered her question to the teacher, a Mr. McGoohan, whom she didn't know.

Tip had been absent. On Friday, as well as yesterday.

In the cafeteria at lunchtime that news stirred Gail to decision. "There's no point chewing your fingernails and imagining disasters. Scott came in the Moby Dick today, so we'll drive up there after school and bang on the door. OK?"

"Sure. Why not?" Scott Gassler stretched his long legs out and folded his arms across his chest. "Personally, I don't understand all the fuss. I'll eat my track shoes if you find him with his hair even mussed. He's not about to damage himself, and he probably trots off to the doctor every time he sneezes. He likes himself too much."

Corry opened her mouth, then closed it again. Even if she knew how to explain about Tip's paper bag, she couldn't do it. Not even to make Scott like him better. It was private. Period.

After school Corry and Gail met Scott by the Moby Dick down in the student parking lot. Five minutes later they were turning up the steep drive from Elysian Way. Scott pulled up in front of the garage door.

No answer came to Corry's repeated rings of the back doorbell, or Gail's uninhibited banging with the front door-knocker. It was Gail who pushed through the shrubbery to peer in at the garage's side window. "The VW's gone," she announced.

And not only the car. Through a gap in the curtains of the housekeeper's—Tip's—room, Corry saw only a neatly made-up cot and a bare bedside table and desk. No hi-fi. No computer. Already one corner of his Windham Hill poster had curled forlornly away from the wall.

He was gone. Just like that.

Corry fretted her way through dinner wondering what she ought to do, and afterward had a hard time keeping her mind from wandering back to Tip when she was trying to concentrate on homework. Where was he? Was he all right? What had happened? She couldn't even call Information to ask for the Meredith telephone number in New York. She didn't know Tip's father's name, and there could be hundreds of Merediths in New York. Besides, what would she do with a phone number if she had it and could pay her mother for the long-distance charge? Whatever she had to say to Tip, to explain to him, to apologize for, would be hard enough to put into words if he were in the same room, let alone on the dreaded telephone with every tick of the clock costing money.

There were Mr. and Mrs. Frowd, but Corry couldn't bring herself to dial their number. She was a complete stranger to them. They would hardly give her Mr. Meredith's address or phone number unless Tip had mentioned her to them. Somehow she knew he hadn't. He was a great one for keeping things to himself.

Going up to the attic later in the evening, Corry was distracted for a while by cutting a series of tiles from a thin layer of clay rolled out with the old rolling pin. She draped them over the rolling pin to dry, and then began the painstaking process of making separate molds from the cup's foot and bowl. The work went smoothly, but that didn't cheer her.

Nor did the promising results early the next morning of her practice-piping of coral strands like those that twined to make the cup's stem. There was, she decided, only one way of learning what she wanted to know.

She could ask at the nursing home.

She couldn't ask Mrs. Dressler for fear of upsetting her again. But there would be a manager. And at least one of the attendants had seen her on that earlier visit. It was a chance. No harm trying, so long as old Mrs. Dressler didn't catch sight of her and go all wobbly again. . . .

"But I better fasten my hair back off my forehead just

in case—so I don't look so much like Great-Grandma," Corry told Gail over lunch once she had explained her plan.

"I'll come with you," Gail offered. "You have to get off at my bus stop for The Birches anyway." Seeing Corry's doubtful expression, she grinned. "Don't worry, I won't tag along if you don't want me to."

Instead, it was agreed that Gail would come over to do her homework at Corry's house after dinner, and after a short detour to Gail's house for Corry to fasten her frizzle of bangs back with a pair of borrowed combs, Corry went on alone. Arriving at The Birches, she found a moving van parked outside and the nursing home in a quiet bustle of confusion. The deep drone of a carpet-cleaning machine drowned out the conversation in the side parlors, in one of which a family group was visiting. In the other the bridge game of three or four weeks past seemed to be going strong still. A wide strip of plastic had been laid to protect the clean section of carpet, and along it movers wheeled stacks of sealed and labelled cartons out to the porch and their van. In the midst of the confusion a little old lady in a pretty polka-dotted dress and matching sweater clutched her handbag in gloved hands and watched with interest from a straight-backed chair near the foot of the stair. As Corry stood undecided in the middle of the reception hall, a florist's delivery man brushed past her with an arrangement of daffodils and jonquils. A white-uniformed attendant appeared and vanished up the stairs.

Crossing to the old lady, Corry bent to ask where the office was.

"What's that?" The old lady leaned forward. "What's that?"

"Nothing," Corry said hastily, shaking her head. She backed away to let the movers past with a set of box springs, and then moved toward the rear of the hall. She took a quick, nervous look in at the open doors of a television lounge and small library, and read the small brass signs on the others: *Telephone, Dining Room, Nurse,* and *Office.*

She tapped on the door marked *Office.*

A woman's voice answered. "Come in."

Corry opened the door onto a small but pleasant office with a bank of file cabinets, a window looking out onto the sunny garden, fresh flowers on the handsome table that served as a desk, and a comfortable armchair for visitors. A gray-haired woman in a businesslike blue suit sat at the desk, and a large, sandy-haired man in gray filled the armchair.

Corry reddened and took a step backward. "I'm sorry," she said hastily. "I wanted to ask—I'll wait."

The man sat forward. "No, no, don't go. I'm in no hurry. Ask your question."

The woman smiled. "I'm Mrs. Sammire. How can I help you?"

Corry took a deep breath. "I don't want to bother Mrs. Dressler, so I wondered if you could give me her family's address in New York. Her great-grandson's my cousin, but I didn't get to see him before he left. I'm Cordelia Tipson," she added awkwardly, thinking that she should have probably said that first.

Mrs. Sammire looked at the gentleman opposite her as if to say *Excuse me,* and shook her head regretfully. "I'm sorry, Miss—Tipson?—but I would have to check with Mr. Meredith before I could give you an address." She paused. "I take it you didn't know that Mrs. Dressler was leaving us?"

"Leaving?" Corry looked at her, uncomprehending.

"Yes. For New York. A nurse from her new residence there flew out to accompany her on the flight back. They left for the Pittsburgh airport only five or ten minutes ago."

Corry was startled for a moment into stillness. But then she realized what it must mean. Tip was at least a little bit all right. He had kept his promise. Her eyes shone.

"That's great! I mean, her room here was really nice, but—" She broke off, realizing that explanations would be too complicated. "I'd better go. I'm sorry I interrupted."

"I could forward a message, if you like," Mrs. Sammire offered.

"No, that's OK," Corry said, backing out the door. "But maybe later. Thanks again."

As she made her way back along the hall, the ivory-colored, glass-fronted cabinet that had held the china figures and fragile little Lotus bowl passed her on its way out.

I hope it gets there in one piece.

Not just the bowl. Tip too.

Fifteen

"**A**RE YOU GOING to write to him?"
Gail asked as they climbed the attic
stairs. At supper Corry had described her visit to The
Birches, but had given only a vague mumble of an answer
when her mother asked the same question.

"I ought to," Corry said slowly. "To tell him about the
cup and ask about the family papers he says he found in his
attic."

"You don't sound very enthusiastic." Gail gave her a
look of pitying disapproval. "I grant you he was stuck up
and about as much fun as a clothes hanger, but—"

Corry turned quickly. "He *is* fun. And not stuck up,
just—shy."

Gail's eyebrows rose.

"He *is*," Corry said passionately. "Worse than I am.
He's just a lot better at hiding it. And don't say 'was.'
He's—"

"He's what?"

The shadowy, shapeless thought that had been niggling more and more insistently at the back of Corry's mind since she left The Birches was suddenly, sharply clear. Almost absentmindedly she removed the lid from the slip crock and began slowly to stir the slip with an old plastic iced tea spoon. The man in Mrs. Sammire's office. The more she thought about it, the more the way he had watched her reminded her strangely of Tip, though he hadn't at all looked like him. Could he have been—No, that was silly.

"Oh, nothing." She poured slip into a small pitcher. "Anyhow, what's exciting is—you know the pottery equipment I told you about?—well, Mr. Hankins has been zipping around organizing things. Now Don's dad's got the motors for the potter's wheel and ball mill all apart to clean them or whatever, and Mr. Hankins's friend Mr. Ginger is going to check out the kiln." Pouring carefully, she filled the molds for the cup's foot and bowl with slip.

Gail picked up the mended cup gingerly. "This is gorgeous. At least, it *was* gorgeous. What'd you use to fill in these bitty holes?"

"ChinaFix. You put a piece of tape over them on the inside, while it's smooth, then fill in from the rippled side. When it's dry, all's you do is pull off the tape."

"What did your mom say about the kiln and stuff?"

"That she wouldn't have it in the house," Corry said without expression. She poured the excess slip out of each mold, leaving a coating that would dry to a fragile thinness, and turned both molds on their sides to dry. "Because we don't have any fire insurance. I told Mrs. Giorgiadis this afternoon, and she said they could go in her garage, but that's way up on Smithfield Street." She paused, and then went on with a rush of pleasure. "I showed her some sketches of this nutty cake I want to do, and she was more excited than I am."

Corry moved the tray with the molds to the other table. "She was really upset yesterday when I told her Mom wouldn't let me do it for credit."

Gail shrugged. "Because she knows you're good. I bet you're better than anybody in any of the regular art classes. I keep *telling* you, but you don't listen." She peered into the molds but was careful not to touch them. The plaster had already absorbed enough water from the slip that the surface was no longer shiny. "If all this works, what are you going to do with the cups? Try to sell them to gift shops?"

Corry looked up, startled, from the pastry bag she was filling from one of Mr. Hankins's crocks with a much thicker slip. "Gosh, no. That wouldn't be right. Lotus is too special. All I want is for *one* to come out OK. The real cup belonged to Tip's and my great-grandfather as much as to my great-grandma, so it's as much his as mine. He gave me the real one. I'll give this to him. To remember it by."

She adjusted her chair and, picking up the bag again, piped a practise-length of clay coral.

"OK," she said abruptly. "Now's the time, ladies and gentlemen, to shut up and stop breathing."

Placing the lid from a plastic whipped-topping tub beside the bat, and standing the cup before her, she took up the pastry bag again, and began to pipe in earnest. With each controlled hesitation the branch grew a knobble, and with each twist a change of angle. When the branch reached full length, she moved the tube's tip back to add the brief beginning of a twig at one bend, a slightly longer one at the next.

When four strands had been transferred gingerly, one by one, from the bat to the lid, Corry covered them loosely with the tub itself.

"They're so spindly, they'd dry too fast," she explained.

"How do you *do* that?" Gail marveled. "It's like magic."

Corry was pleased with them herself. So much so that it set her to thinking.

Corry woke at five-thirty the next morning and crept up to the attic in her pajamas, keeping close to the wall, where the stair treads were not so likely to creak as she went. When she had untied the molds and eased one half up off the other, she found both foot and bowl perfectly shaped, but marred here and there as the first Reggie-and-Lizzes had been by tiny pinholes. They would probably come out in little black specks in the firing, too. But even more disappointing was a faint blurring of the seashell texture, a difference from the original cup caused, she decided, by the smoothing effect of the original's layer of glaze.

Corry was afraid to take a knife to the inside of the plaster mold to sharpen the detail that way. She would do better to work on the cast pieces themselves. But the state of the stem she had fashioned made even that pointless. The four coral strands had dried too thoroughly, and in the process cracked apart. There was nothing to be done but break stem, foot, and bowl into bits, and chuck them in the scrap-clay crock. She had little but scraps and a cup or so of slip left, and even less of the piping clay.

By breakfast time she had poured another foot and bowl, piped four more coral branches onto a bat, tiptoed down to dress for school, and returned to find the delicate, knobbly strands dried just enough to handle. Moistening and then pressing them lightly but firmly together with slip for glue, she twisted the four strands into a shallow spiral similar to the one they would hold on the finished stem, and transferred them to the plastic topping tub's lid. Covering it with the tub, this time she snapped it on tight.

—And ended in having to race, toast in hand, to catch the bus.

During homeroom period Corry got a library pass, and when she passed Gail in the hall on the way to her first period class, she was so preoccupied that she bumped into her and went on without noticing. But the preoccupation did not last.

Tip was back. Corry first saw him after second period, vanishing into his Latin classroom, and chafed with curiosity and impatience until lunchtime. She raced downstairs to the cafeteria, hoping to reach the door in time to catch him on the way in, but he was already in line at least ten people ahead of her.

Corry hesitated. She wanted to dart past all ten and slip into place behind him so there would be no chance of coming through the line and finding him at a filled-up table. But she couldn't. If she had known all ten. . . . But she didn't and she couldn't. Meeting and talking to or making phone calls to more-or-less strangers was one thing. But the very thought of pushing past ten frowns and risking a tenfold argument made her stomach tighten. She might have dared it even so, but—jumping lines was really rude. Besides, the line wasn't all that long, and there were plenty of empty tables. And Annie Corso was up there, third in line behind Tip. Corry knew that if she jumped the line, Annie would have it halfway around the junior class in no time that the Mouse was chasing the Iceberg. The thought of being teased about it was chilling. Even Tike Persons's friendly teasing alarmed her. She was never quite sure how to take it.

She stayed in line.

When she carried her tray away from the cashier, craning to see where Tip might be, she spied him sitting alone at the end of one of the far tables. All that dithering for nothing. And why, for Pete's sake, couldn't she have gone up the line, asking if anyone minded—that she wanted to eat with her cousin? Even if someone had been bad-tempered enough to grumble that, yes, he minded, she could have gone up, asked Tip to save her a seat, and returned to her own place in line. *Next time,* she thought. Next time.

Tip turned his head as Corry approached, and his face lit up. *Like having someone turn on the porch light for you,* Corry thought in relief. She had been terrified that he might have resented her evasiveness since their picnic.

"Where have you *been?*" she demanded as she set down her tray. "Gail and Scott and I went up to the house on Monday and all your stuff was gone."

"Not gone." Tip grinned. "Only stowed in the closet so prowlers peering in the window wouldn't be tempted."

"But where were you?"

"In New York." He leaned across the table to say eagerly, "You remember I asked whether you'd like to go through some old papers?"

Corry nodded.

"Well, in with all the pottery account books and catalogs, I found thirty years' worth of Great-Grandfather's own journals—from 1893 when he left K.T. & K. to start his own pottery, up to 1925, when your great-grandmother died. It was all in this padlocked wooden crate, as if he'd either wanted to shut it away for good, or at least keep it private."

"But why?" Corry swallowed hurriedly, and washed a mouthful of pizza down with a sip of milk. "What was in them?"

Tip, when he had taken a bite of his own pizza, went on as if he had not heard. "Anyway, when I'd read them, I knew there must be more. If you've been keeping a journal for thirty years, chances are you don't give up the habit. And since he married my great-grandmother in 1926, I guessed that any he'd written after that had gone to New York with them in '29. They could have been lost or destroyed when Great-Grandfather died and Great-Grandmother sold their house and moved to the apartment. But I thought that if she put any of the good furniture in storage instead of selling it, Great-Grandfather's books and papers might have gone with it."

"And you went to New York to look for them? Not because you were angry with me?"

"With you? What for?" Tip looked at her blankly, and then reddened. "No, I thought it was the other way around."

"Gosh, no," Corry said quickly. "But what about New York? You went all that way on just a guess? There must be *dozens* of storage companies there. Or—did you ask your dad?"

"Not exactly," Tip said. "But if there *were* family papers in storage, I knew Dad would have a record of them in his computer at home. He's got files on everything from the number of towels at home and at the laundry to the birthdays of everybody he's ever met. But you can't get into that computer by phone. I had to go. Besides—" He grinned. "I was getting nervous. He'd been home almost two weeks, and I was afraid if he didn't find out what I'd done until school was out, the explosion would blow me from here to Kansas City."

It was on the tip of Corry's tongue to ask about old Mrs. Dressler and the tall man in the gray suit, but they could wait. "Go on," she urged with a look at her watch. The bell for the next lunch period would ring in seven minutes.

"It was Thursday night when I decided to go," Tip said. "I left at six Friday morning and drove straight through —except for hamburger stops. It must have been eight when I got in. Just at dark. The rent for my mother's parking-building space is paid up until the end of the year, so I left the VW there and took a taxi home."

Corry drew in her breath nervously. "What'd your dad say?"

"He was out. Just as well, too. I was so tired I couldn't have explained worth peanuts. When I hit the bed I was out like I'd blown a fuse. And since when Dad came in it never occurred to him to look in my room, when he got up the next morning and got a whiff of toast and coffee, he came out armed with a croquet mallet in case I was a hungry burglar."

"But what about Great-Grandfather's journals?" Corry urged impatiently.

"I'd already found them," Tip said. "They were filed as *LHT Archives*—LHT for Lucas Henry Tipson—in the personal property file for Great-Grandmother. The file entry said they were in the storeroom right there in our apartment. And they were. The journals, old letters, photographs, travel souvenirs—a whole footlocker full. When I put it all together with what I knew from the earlier journals, it all made an unhappy kind of sense."

The earlier journals, Tip explained, were simply diary jottings for most of the years between 1893 and 1925: *Went to church, spoke to Miss R. . . . Ran into J.P., still grumbling, on the Diamond. . . . Had a word with Miss R's father, a sensible enough fellow when sober. . . . At nine-fifteen this evening, in a shower of fireworks, Miss Ross accepted my offer of marriage. Jack C., silly fellow, insists the Roman Candles and waterfalls were fired off in honor of the Glorious Fourth, and not Cordelia's decision. . . .*

Though most of the entries were matter-of-fact, it had not been difficult to read between the lines Lucas Henry's deepening devotion to his Cordelia and the harmony and trust that grew between them as their son John grew through childhood and youth to young manhood. It was with the entries that followed upon Cordelia's death in 1925 from influenza that a change came. As Lucas Henry's grief and despair faded, he grew restless, and spoke of the house on Fourth Street being haunted with memories. He would build a new house and give the old to John, who was twenty-three, and a manager in one of his father's potteries. But when the new house was built, Lucas found the loneliness harder to bear than memories. Twelve hours or more a day at one pottery or the other still left too many empty hours.

And then, on New Year's Eve, a Miss Halley appeared like a comet in his sky. A guest at a dinner party given by friends, she paid a pretty compliment to a new Tipson Potteries' luncheon set design. *Praise indeed*, Lucas Henry wrote in his journal. Intrigued at once and soon smitten, the fifty-six-year-old Lucas had proposed, been accepted, and was wed to twenty-nine-year-old Gwendolyn before the month was out. On the day after Christmas of 1926, his second son, Alexander, was born.

Unhappily, from the day of the wedding a coolness had grown up between Lucas and John. John, it was said, had spoken rudely to Gwendolyn—a harsh comment she refused to repeat for fear of making trouble between father and son. Another time, he spoke slightingly in her presence of the work of Tipson Potteries's chief designer, calling his best work "fit only for carnival prizes." Even when John was allowed a chance to prove his own design skill, and—after the company's reorganization—was given management of the Pelican Pottery division, it seemed he would not mind his tongue or mend his ways. By Gwendolyn's report, he ignored repeated invitations to dinner and repeatedly turned a cold shoulder to his father's wife in public.

Though deeply offended, Lucas could bring himself neither to confront his son and condemn his arrogance, nor to punish it by discharging him from the pottery and the family together. Once, indeed, it had seemed as if Gwendolyn were proposing exactly that, but Lucas had misunderstood. It was Gwendolyn who, most considerately, suggested that John's resentment would surely vanish if he felt he were no longer standing in his father's shoes. Why not allow him to *buy* the Pelican works? Yet when that had been accomplished, the rift appeared to widen even further. Before long, Gwendolyn was venturing that perhaps a separation for a time would help. If she and Lucas and Alexander were out of the way—if they were to go to New York for a season—John could truly stand on his own two feet.

And so they had gone. And what with one thing and another, somehow never came back.

Corry stopped, stricken, outside the cafeteria door. "Then—it was all my grandpa's fault?"

"No, *no*," Tip said quickly. He moved to the door that led out onto the hillside and opened it. "That's what was so awful. It was all lies. All Great-Grandmother. She may have been ferociously jealous to start with, but the lies didn't start until after Alexander—*my* grandfather—was born. Since her little Sandy couldn't look out for his own interests, she would. And the more of his father's love—and wealth—he had, the better. And there was quite a bit of money. Great-Grandfather was one of the lucky few who lost nothing. The stock market crashed before he had a chance to invest the money from the sale of the potteries in stocks. And then, with everyone trying frantically to sell property and nobody buying, he was able to purchase a house in midtown Manhattan and several good business rental properties for peanuts, and squirrel away enough to live on. They had to scrimp, but Great-Grandmother must have known how valuable the property would be once the Depression was over."

Corry followed Tip outside. "But how do you know all that? Are you just guessing?"

Tip thrust his hands in his pockets. "There was an old lockbox in with the journals and papers. I know it was Great-Grandmother's, and I had no right, but I fiddled it open. There were twenty or thirty letters in it, all from John to his father, and all unopened."

Corry stared. "She *hid* them?"

Tip nodded. "She never even read them. Why she didn't burn them is the real puzzle. It felt eerie opening them. The first ones are dated just after the move to New York, and the last one was sent just before the Pelican Pottery closed. You can tell that poor John still hadn't figured out what was going on. There's this bewildered *What-have-I-done?* tone in all of them, but the same queer Tipson pride keeps him from asking straight out what's wrong. He says things like 'I know that you and Gwen like to keep to yourselves, but—' and 'If you do come back for a visit, we'll have an old-fashioned family dinner—something I've missed these past few years.' "

"That sounds like . . . like he was never *invited* to all those dinner parties he never turned up at," Corry said in astonishment.

"Exactly. And once you read the letters and go back over Great-Grandfather's journals, a lot of things stick out like billboards. Nothing ever *did* happen directly between the two of them. It was all Great-Grandmother digging moats and building walls. A word here, a word there—and all done with great charm. Your grandpa never had a chance."

Corry bit her lip. "Maybe. But they *let* it happen if they didn't either of them say what they really felt. Like, 'Why did you say that to her? It hurt me,' or, 'Why've you been so cold and polite? It hurts.' "

Tip looked out across the house-clad, tree-green hills. "Why were you avoiding me last week? That hurt."

Corry felt as if her tongue would cleave to the roof of her mouth and that her throat would close. But with her eyes fixed on her shoes, and her heart thumping, she managed, awkwardly and haltingly, to say what she had longed for days to say.

"It's. . . . You scared me. I've never felt for anybody, not yet anyhow, the way you want—wanted—me to feel for you. I'm not ready for all that. But I was afraid if I said so, you'd be too hurt to be friends. I didn't know what to do." She looked up anxiously. "I'm not Cordelia."

Tip swallowed, and when he smiled Corry wasn't sure whether it was his own smile or the paper bag's.

"Back to Square One, then?"

Corry nodded, her own smile lighting up her eyes. "Square One." And then she jumped. "Oh, gosh—the bell!"

They raced up the stairs, Tip talking all the way, and lingered for a moment outside Mr. Harmill's room. Tip's father, it seemed, waking late on Saturday morning to that aroma of toast and coffee, had been surprised to see Tip but not in the least surprised by the tale of the well-planned flight from Litchfield Academy. His secretary, proofreading the original letters as they were entered on her computer terminal, had been faintly suspicious—just enough to send copies to Mr. Meredith's Hong Kong hotel. The telegraphed reply had directed her to check with the Frowds and, if Tip really was attending school, to do nothing.

"He was going to turn up as soon as he had a free weekend and come down on me like a ton of bricks," Tip said. "For hacking into the company computer more than anything else. But I don't think he was as angry as he pretended to be. He said he hadn't thought I had that much initiative. Anyhow, he actually sat down and listened for a change. And he felt really bad about Great-Grandmother, and said he'd take care of it. He's sure Mother didn't have any more idea than he had that Great-Grandmother disliked Ohio so much, and—" He broke off reluctantly as the second bell was about to ring. "Look, I've got to run. See you next period."

In the five minutes before Mrs. Giorgiadis's class, and the five between art appreciation and anatomy, the rest of Tip's tale tumbled out. When he left for New York, he had

205

had mixed feelings about returning to East Liverpool, but his father gave him no choice. The end of the school year was too close. And there were penalties, too: no car, and no credit card. Mrs. Frowd would be paid to keep the freezer and pantry stocked, but with an allowance of only ten dollars a week and lunch money, Tip could no longer afford to pay her to do his laundry. ("Don't look at me!" Corry said in mock alarm.)

A new arrangement for Mrs. Dressler—in a Manhattan apartment-residence for the elderly—had been made on Monday, and on Tuesday Mr. Meredith's secretary, after several long-distance telephone calls, had located a mover who could send a van to The Birches on Wednesday. On Wednesday morning Tip and his father had flown out together from New York.

"And that was that," Tip finished as they headed down the stairs after sixth period. He sounded impressed with his father's efficiency in spite of himself.

"Did you—" Corry hesitated. "Did you tell him about Mom and me?"

"Sort of." He tried to hide his blush with a grin. "But only that I'd met you. If he thought I had more on my mind than family history and school, I might've had to stay in New York and go to summer classes instead. This way I still get to go to Italy to stay with Mother for the summer."

"Did you show him the picture of Cordelia's portrait?" Corry asked. "Because if you did, I think he knows who I am. There was this man in the office at The Birches yesterday afternoon—big, sandy-haired, and a—a sort of watching look. Was that him?" She explained about her visit to the nursing home.

"That was Dad." Tip shook his head in wonder. "He didn't say Word One to me."

"Sounds like that makes two of you," Corry observed as she pushed open the anatomy lab door. "And where've I heard it before?"

Tip went to his lab-station wearing a thoughtful look.

Sixteen

THURSDAY KEPT ON being a good day all day. Not even Mr. Harmill's reminder about the algebra quiz to come on Monday could spoil it.

Arriving home, Corry hurried straight up to the attic. She was on her way back down with the tiles that were to go to the Potters' Supply for firing when Mr. Hankins came out onto the landing to pass on the latest news from Brian McCloskey: The sale of the house *had* fallen through, and the garage was Corry's to use until another buyer turned up. Mr. Hankins's friend Ralph Ginger had very kindly gone over on his lunch hour to take a look at the kiln and reported that aside from the heating coils, which needed replacing, it was in fairly good shape. And he had offered to see whether he could find the coils it needed that very afternoon while he was up in Pittsburgh.

Corry was so elated that it did not occur to her until

she had been all the way down to the Potters' Supply and back that she should have stopped at Mason Color and Chemical to see about getting more feldspar for a new batch of the clay body. She needed more ball clay from the Kentucky-Tennessee Clay Company representative, too. Better to make more clay body now than run out after she had mastered the firing process and was casting the rest of the Reggie-and Lizzes. It was only four-thirty. She *could* make another trip. But there were so many other things she needed to do. . . .

There was always the telephone, of course. Step One: Look up the number. Step Two: Pick up the receiver. Step Three—

Corry froze in alarm when Mrs. Higbee answered on the first ring (Step Three: Decide how you're going to say what you're going to say before you dial the number?), but she managed surprisingly well. Afterward she called and left a message for the clay company's Mr. Franz about the ball clay. Maybe just because they *were* business, business calls weren't so bad. When you ran out of things you needed to say, you said "Goodbye" instead of limping along trying to sound interested and interesting.

Mrs. Higbee had been vague when Corry asked about the cost, but even if she had to pay for all her materials from now on, she would manage somehow. Get a summer job even if it was just fastening on price tags at Murphy's or sweeping floors at the supermarket. Even borrow from Don, like he said. Or Tip.

When she finished telephoning, the sound of the TV drew Corry from the hall into the living room, where she found her mother with her feet up on the sofa and a cup of tea and plate of cookies beside her on the TV table. Next to the plate lay a key on a peculiar key-chain, a battered blue-enamelled disk with a light-blue "√" in the center.

"Mr. Hankins says that's for you," April Tipson announced. "He said you'd know what it was for."

Mr. McCloskey's garage.

Corry covered the five blocks to the garage off Seventh Street in what seemed nothing flat. The Yale lock on the side door was stiff from disuse, but after a frustrating moment she fiddled it open and stepped into the cool shadows.

As she groped for the light switch on the wall between the door and window, Corry noticed and vaguely wondered at a familiar piney odor surprising in a place of dust and clay and a hard-packed earthen floor with a great, dark patch of ancient oil. The old car, she was glad to see, was gone. And so too, as she saw when she had flipped the light switch, were the dust and cobwebs she had expected. The windows shone. The sink and the work counters along the end and far walls were scrubbed clean. The shelves and the jars and boxes of setters and other kilnware that lined them had been dusted. And the walls. To be so clean, the rough plank walls must have been vacuumed; the earthen floor was swept smooth as concrete. Kiln and wheel and the old ball mill were as clean as brush and sponge and scouring powder could make them.

And Grandpa Tipson's modeling tools were set out in a neat row on the worktable under the window opposite.

Corry stood in the middle of the floor, hugging herself

210

in delight and excitement, and shivering a little in awe. Though Tip might discover the past in the writings and artifacts it left strewn behind it in the present, in this place it was alive still. Not in the tools. In her. If she made one piece worth the making, it was Mr. Hankins's and old Mr. McCloskey's and her grandfather and great-grandfather's and Joshua Poole's doing too. And all those English potters who'd sailed so far from home to find the work their hands hungered for.

"C'mon, aren't you even gonna say 'Omigosh!'?"

The spell broken, Corry wheeled to find her mother, grinning, arms folded, leaning against the door frame.

"Oh, Mom!" Corry ran to fling her arms around her. "It's wonderful. But it must have taken you all day. Your whole day off!"

"That's OK." Mrs. Tipson disentangled herself. Her tone was offhanded, but Corry could tell that she was pleased. "It was kind of a challenge. I borrowed Donna Chappick's shopping cart—that collapsible thing—to wheel all the cleaning stuff over. I thought there'd be time to move more of your pottery junk over, but I decided to call it quits at four."

Corry gave her mother a quick, puzzled look. "Why'd you do it? I mean, you said I was wasting too much time on potting already." Her mother wasn't one to change her mind, so it must mean *some*thing.

"That's why," Mrs. Tipson said drily. She shrugged. "From now till summer vacation you won't get over here much except weekends and maybe an hour or so after

211

school. By the time you finish your homework after supper, there won't be time to get over and back before dark. And I'm not gonna have you traipsing across town *after* dark."

"Even if Don comes with me?" Corry ventured.

"I didn't think of that," her mother said grumpily, hiding a flicker of—amusement? Impatience? Corry wasn't sure.

"I still got the shopping cart over home," Mrs. Tipson said as she moved to leave. "You get a move on, you oughta be able to bring a load or two over before suppertime."

Two loads. Corry took the crocks, Mr. Hankins's bowl, the contents of the pigeonholes, the Reggie-and-Liz mold, an almost-empty sack of plaster, and the chair, since there was nothing in the garage to sit on. The cup-makings and the four fragile greenware figurines she left behind. They would have to be packed carefully and carried separately, along with the greenware cup when it was ready.

The day's best came last. After Corry finished plodding through her evening's homework and spent fifteen minutes fiddling intently with scissors and cardboard, she climbed to the almost bare attic room where the two molds and the upside-down plastic bowl sat waiting. Opening the molds for the foot and bowl, she found the castings perfect except for several pinholes which vanished under the careful touch of a small brush dipped in water. When she unsnapped the plastic bowl covering the cup's half-made stem the "coral" strands were firm but still plastic. With the photograph as a model, Corry gently twined them together, at the one end curving each down along the cup's foot, fastening it there with slip and careful pressure. The most delicate job of all

212

was nestling the bowl of the cup securely in the coral branches. The cut-out cardboard supports she had made held the bowl's slight weight from straining the new joins or buckling the branches before they dried.

She sat back on the old trunk and looked at the cup with a shiver of excitement that made her feel as if she were full of static electricity from her toes to the ends of her hair. Oh, as a copy of an artist's—old Lucas Henry's?—masterpiece, it might deserve no more than a B or even B—, but as itself it was still amazing. *She* had made *that!*

Don was back in school the next day, Friday, but Corry was so intent on using every scrap of time at lunch and between classes to get a head start on the weekend's homework that she had no chance to say much to him, or to Tip, except an excited hint that there might be something interesting to see at the McCloskey garage on Sunday afternoon. Her high spirits survived even a stint at the blackboard in algebra class, and as the school bus made its way down into town she marveled at how much greener the grass and hedges seemed to have grown in one sunny spring day, and how much more thickly leaved the trees were. Even the most weatherbeaten houses looked less gray and desolate.

She got off at the stop before her own and cut down to Second Street to pick up the test tiles that had been fired in the Potters' Supply kiln. Though they looked all right at first glance, they lacked the true Lotus translucence, and a test on the kitchen table with a smart tap from a spoon proved them too brittle as well. So 2350 degrees was still not hot enough.

213

A few minutes later, Mr. Hankins came downstairs with the garage key—she had returned it to him so that he could let Mr. Ginger in to replace the broken and rusty coils in the kiln—and they went over to the old garage together. Mr. Hankins repeated everything Mr. Ginger had told him and everything he himself remembered about firing and cooling rates, and Corry wrote it all down. The kiln was similar to the one at school, but larger, and had both a pyrometer to measure the heat and an automatic cut-off that could be set to turn the kiln off at whatever final temperature she chose.

"I'm going to try it slower than my art teacher did at school," Corry said nervously. "If I start really early tomorrow morning, it can be finished and turned off before suppertime."

Everything seemed to go so well at first. With old Mr. McCloskey's kiln furniture she built up a shelf inside the kiln that would put her new test tiles at the very center of the kiln space—but then rebuilt it three inches lower. She could not bear the thought of succeeding and then having to wait a week to fire the cup. Even if she wanted to fire up on Sunday, she couldn't. Not with church service at ten-thirty. She couldn't go away and leave the kiln going full blast. Not when she was responsible for the garage. Because of their own house's old wiring, her mother was fiercely strict about never leaving the oven—or even the clothes-washer—on when they were out. And in the wintertime you didn't even leave the *room* without turning off the kerosene heater. Besides, if the kiln blew a fuse she needed to be right there to put in a new one before the heat dropped and her cup was ruined. She knew where the fuse box was and had brought an extra fuse from home.

She placed the cup at the center of the ceramic shelf—which she had remembered to paint with alumina so the base of the cup would not stick when it vitrified—closed and latched the heavy door, set the cut-off at 2375 degrees, closed her eyes and flipped the switch to ON.

The morning went quickly enough. Corry finished her homework, going through the algebra problems twice—a practice that had become a habit. Then there was a letter to write, which she labored over long and carefully. After a picnic lunch of a peanut butter and jelly sandwich, an apple, and a warmish grape soda, she settled down to reread the chapter on glazing in *The Complete Book of Pottery Making*. By three when she opened the small peephole in the side of the kiln for the nineteenth or twentieth time, the dull glow had brightened to a cherry-red. The hour until four crept along slowly, and that until five more slowly still. A little before six, as the yellow brilliance visible through the peephole began, above 2200 degrees, to shade itself into a white too bright to look at, Corry had one last glimpse of the cup, a pale, fiery golden marvel almost indistinguishable from the heat that surrounded it, before she was forced to look away. For a good five minutes, everywhere she looked a brilliant fiery-white disk burned in the middle of her vision. She didn't dare look again. And yet . . . the cup had seemed

—shorter. Blurred. It had to be a trick of the heat. The tiles had remained as sharp-edged as ever when fired at 2350 degrees.

As the pyrometer edged up past 2350 degrees, Corry bit at a fingernail and fought the temptation to look in again at the peephole. What if 2375 degrees were that one degree too hot?

Glass did melt. . . .

"I chickened out and shut it off at 2365," Corry said miserably. "I knew 2350 degrees wasn't hot enough, and I figured just fifteen degrees more would be safe. But it went *phloop!* anyhow. I saw when I came over this morning for a peep in the peephole. I can't figure what I did wrong."

Don tugged the kiln's heavy door open, and Tip, who had turned up at church and happily accepted Mrs. Tipson's invitation to Sunday lunch afterwards, reached in to lift out the cup.

"Oh, gosh!" He almost whispered it as he saw what Corry had seen through the peephole earlier. "Oh Cor, I'm sorry."

The cup's brief, blazing loveliness was gone. The weight of the shell-thin bowl had bowed the stem as it vitrified. And as the stem buckled, melting, the bowl had dropped like a wilted, misshapen flower.

Don cocked his head at Corry. "You're taking it pretty calmly, aren't you? No bleak despair, no clutching at your middle?"

Corry seemed not to hear. Going to the window, she held the cup up and spread the fingers of her other hand between it and the light. Shadow fingers moved behind the wilted seashell-flower's white bisque surface.

"Look, you can see through it! And it didn't melt all that much, so the temperature must've been almost right." She scowled. "But I did something wrong. I must have. I've got to find *out* so I can try again next Saturday. I—" She broke off as Tip gave a nod toward the doorway.

"Hey, Mr. Hankins!" Don said cheerfully. "Come on in and see the body."

"Body?" The old gentleman looked startled. "Oh, the unfortunate cup. Your mother told me, Corry. I've brought you a visitor who may be able to help."

The visitor—a tall, solid, balding man who for all Corry could tell might have been anywhere between fifty and sixty—was Ralph Ginger. From his name and something in the way Mr. Hankins had spoken of his "young friend," Corry had imagined someone red-haired, youngish and earnest, not a hearty, booming, man in a pink shirt and Madras plaid slacks.

"Your mother told us you had come over just for a look, not to work," Mr. Hankins said with his careful politeness once he had made his introductions and Corry had introduced Tip. "So I thought we wouldn't be interrupting you. Mr. Ginger—Ralph—has been telling me a few things about porcelain—bone-china to be precise—that I hadn't known. I think they may be helpful to you."

"There!" Mr. Ginger boomed unexpectedly, pointing at the wilted cup in Corry's hand. "There's what I was telling you about, George. You didn't know because Albert always worked with lower-firing whiteware."

217

He stabbed a finger at the cup. "That's how your vitrified body'll deform without support. If the heat had gone higher, this would have melted down like the Wicked Witch of the West. Left a nice little puddle of glass. . . . Here, now!" He interrupted himself to cross to the worktable, where he bent down to take a close look at the greenware Reggie-and-Lizzes. Turning, he gave Corry a sharp look.

"This your work? Gloryosky! And I was expecting something cute. Good, but kid-stuff. I should have put more trust in George's judgment. These are really fine. *Really* fine. And you've even managed that piped-on filigree. I'd like to have seen that whatsis you've got there. What was it? A cup? It must've been a dinger."

"Thank you." Corry flushed at the praise, but for once her shyness was forgotten. "What kind of support?" she asked eagerly. "You mean propping it up? How? The book I got out of the library doesn't tell about porcelains, so I didn't know. What *do* you do?"

Simple. Bury it in calcined alumina or flint in a sagger. Simple once you knew, that is. Mr. Ginger had, he said, two good books, *Pottery Production Processes* and *Fine Ceramics: Technology and Applications*, that he would lend her. And those tiny black specks on the bisque cup? Iron in the casting slip. Modern production methods used magnetic separators to get it out, but the early makers of bone china had been plagued with the specks. He would look up some 180- or 200-mesh screen so that she could give the remaining slip a good straining. She had a lot to learn, but he was impressed. Yes indeed.

. . .

218

"I've got enough sagger clay to make the sagger," Corry said intently when Mr. Hankins and Mr. Ginger had left. "It'll have to be deeper than the frit one, but it doesn't have to be that wide. If I make it now, it'll dry soon enough to get it fired by Friday easy. OK—everybody out."

"Oh come on," Don said. "We can do the wedging."

"On second thought—" Tip put in hastily as Corry reached for the stumpy old broom in the corner with a determined light in her eye, "maybe we can't."

Seventeen

*T*HE FOLLOWING WEEK went by in a rush: Algebra quiz, taking the sagger to be fired, mixing and double-screening the new clay body, making test tiles from it, casting and piping a new cup, picking up—and insisting, red-cheeked, on paying for —ten pounds of ground flint, and double-scrubbing Mr. Hankins's crocks and dipping bowl for the glaze. Not to speak of homework. And—almost as gratifying as her work on the cup—for what was the third week in a row, Corry's algebra quiz score had inched upward, passing D+ at last, coming within a hair of a glorious C—. Apparently the less time she had to worry, the better she did.

On Tuesday afternoon, when Corry was to make the new casting of the cup's foot and bowl and pipe the pieces of the new stem, Tip rode the No. 20 bus down with her and came to watch "his" cup in the making. But, she made clear, on Saturday when the new cup went into the kiln and on Sunday when it came out, there was to be no audience. "So if anything goes wrong I can storm around and smash things instead of being all noble and patient," Corry joked. But it was really because she knew that everyone else—Tip especially—would be more disappointed than she would. The impatience that made her risk a cup when a test tile would have done, her curiosity about the *why?* of each flaw or failure, and her eagerness to try again made the disappointment a fleeting thing. Then too, she wanted to increase the firing time, making a long watch longer. Since the cup would be buried in flint and all that would be visible through the peephole was the side of the sagger, keeping watch on the firing would be about as interesting as watching grass grow.

Even with everything else, Corry found time—though it meant walking down the long hill home—to go to the house on Elysian Way on Wednesday after school to help Tip take the painting of Cordelia from its frame and painstakingly to remove the tacks that fastened the canvas to its wooden stretcher. They rolled the canvas loosely and fitted it into a long, fat mailing tube that Tip had brought from New York so that when he went home to pack for his summer in Italy he could take Cordelia along to be restored. And summer vacation was just over two weeks away.

Saturday was as long as Corry had expected. Longer. And then on Sunday afternoon when the pyrometer showed that the long, slow cool-down was complete and she wrenched the heavy door open, Corry found the flint in the sagger still hot to the touch. Caution won out over curiosity.

221

She left the door ajar and went away. After supper, with a promise to her mother to take a look and come straight home, she returned to the old garage.

Wrestling the heavy sagger out and taking it to a clear stretch of worktable, Corry used her fingers to scoop out the still-warm flint until the cup's rim was clear. Then she tipped and propped the sagger so that she could scoop more freely. With half the flint cleared away, she righted the sagger and lifted the bisque cup free.

There was a faint mark that might be a hairline crack where one coral branch joined the seashell bowl, but glaze could seal and strengthen that. Otherwise the cup was—to Corry's great surprise—quite perfect. The transformation from clay to china seemed almost magical. Not hard work. Not chemistry. Magic!

Thursday was Glazing Day. When Mr. Hankins let it be known that he wouldn't in the least mind, and in fact would count it a privilege to be on hand, Corry's impulsive hug and "Yes, please!" turned him pink with pleasure. Hurrying home after school to change into her workclothes, she found him waiting in the downstairs hall in his, a small carton under his arm, ready to go.

And he understood the impatience that had decided her on using the cup for the first glaze test. He would have done the same himself. But he suggested that since it was important to learn what was exactly the right thickness of glaze, she might do a few tiles, too, each with a slightly different thickness, marking each tile with a note of the weight per pint. He had brought his own old viscosity gauge which, floated upright in the glaze, would tell just that. For the last half block, he was almost trotting.

When the glaze was mixed, sieved, "weighed" with the gauge, and a bit more water added to bring it to precisely thirty ounces to the pint, it was much thicker than Corry would have guessed. Mr. Hankins had never worked with vitrified ware, but knew that because it would not absorb moisture from the glaze as a low-firing clay would, a too-thin mixture would run off or adhere unevenly.

A part of the mixture went into the dipping bowl and the remainder into one of the crocks to be covered carefully and stored. Then Corry, nervous but intent, dipped the first curved tile just as Mr. Hankins showed her, holding it across the back with fingers and thumb, and with a turn of her wrist skimming its surface across the glaze. A bit too thick, Mr. Hankins thought, and Corry added and stirred in what seemed like a very small amount of water to make any difference, skimmed another tile, and then at Mr. Hankins's nod added a bit more water, and skimmed a third. The third looked right to Mr. Hankins. Corry took a deep breath, dipped the tips of her fingers into the glaze, picked up the cup and, following Mr. Hankins's directions, held it with two fingers on the base and two on the rim and "walked" them around the cup so that it revolved in the glaze. After tipping it upright to be sure the bottom of the bowl was covered, she inverted it for several moments to drain, then set it down on one of the small, three-pronged ceramic stands called a "stilt."

Corry's eyes shone. Forgetting the glaze on her fingers, she reached out solemnly to shake Mr. Hankins's hand. He laughed—a surprisingly booming laugh of sheer pleasure. Then they washed their hands, locked up, and went home.

When Tip arrived at five on Saturday afternoon, carrying two six-packs of root beer and an odd, oblong canvas case, he found Don, four folding Chappick porch chairs, and a bowl of Mrs. Chappick's potato salad had arrived before him. Corry had made a chocolate fudge cake, and Gail showed up at six with ketchup, mustard, eight fat hamburgers and her tape deck.

"I told Scott to take his mom to a movie," she announced. "This is the first Saturday night we haven't gone out since I went to Virginia Beach last summer with my folks. It feels kind of nice. Weird, but nice."

Because of the cake, Corry hadn't been able to fire up as early as she had planned, but since the glaze, or "glost" firing, as Mr. Hankins called it, was done at a temperature about two hundred and forty degrees lower than the bisque firing, she hoped to reach the shut-off at about nine-thirty. By eleven-thirty—midnight at the very latest—the kiln should be cool enough for them to have a look. She would *have* to see whether the cup was still standing. How could she go to bed not knowing whether it had survived or blown itself to bits?

By seven-thirty, when the last crumb of cake vanished, the dull glow visible through the kiln's peephole had ripened to a murky red and the cup, red too, had the unreal look of an object seen in a darkroom's red light.

"Like the poisoned chalice in the fire-dragon's cave in *Netherworld*," Don intoned in a sepulchral voice.

"Don't *say* that," Corry exclaimed. "That one got smashed to bits!"

The kiln chamber brightened slowly as they talked and played the tapes, shading through cherry to a bright red and on through orange-red to a bright orange by nine o'clock. As it began to pale toward white-orange and Corry's eye winced at the bright peephole, she remembered how the brilliance a week before had seared the peephole's circle on her vision, and took one last, quick look. Then she closed the peephole, squeezed her eyes tight shut, and crossed her fingers.

"What's in the bag?" Don asked idly.

Tip grinned. "Our great-grandfather's camping cot and my space blanket. I decided that by midnight I wasn't going to be in the mood for hiking back up the hill. I thought, if it's OK with you, Corry, I could just sack out here and go home in the morning."

"Without a bathroom? Gosh, no," Corry said. "You can set it up in our front hall. Or the living room."

"Is it one of those old-fashioned canvas-and-toothpick things?" Don asked. "Forget it. Putting them up's like working some kind of nutty puzzle. You might as well sleep on a floor—it'll land you there anyhow. Why don't I just drive you on up in Dad's car?"

"Or I can," offered Gail, who had driven down in her mother's car. "As long as I still get home by midnight."

Experiment proved Don right about the cot. After twenty minutes of vain attempts it did stand on its own six legs at last, and Tip eased himself down onto the tautly-stretched canvas. But the cross-legged cot was simply waiting until he put his arms behind his head and crossed his ankles to collapse.

Tip, who had begun to be a little more at ease, more himself, was embarrassed. "There has to be a trick to it," he said as he bundled it back into the canvas bag. "Or else it's missing a part. I think it's the one Great-Grandfather must have used when the Forest and Stream Club camped out."

Neither Gail nor Don had heard of the old Forest and Stream Hunting and Fishing Club, and as Corry drew one story and then another from Tip, before long his paper bag had completely vanished, and the others were listening to the old tales in delight.

"They really fed the poor horse *whiskey?*" Gail asked in disbelief.

"I swear. They got the owner to come out after it with a wagon, but it surprised them all by staggering back to town on its own four legs."

Don leaned forward, entranced. "The guy who rode the cow from camp to church—did you say they called him Mongo? That was my great-grandad's nickname. Short for Montgomery. Wallace Montgomery, my mom's grandad. You ought to write all this stuff down. I bet nobody else remembers it."

"You know—" Corry sat up with a surprised look. "You know all those journals and papers you waded through, and how you go zipping around looking things up and tracking things down to make sense out of something? You ought to be a historian. You really should. I never used to think knowing all that history stuff mattered, but it does.

I mean—the past isn't really *past*. It goes on niggling away all the time. Pushing people this way and that. Keeping them apart. But maybe if they understood what went on before, they could do better. I mean—" She flushed. "I don't know what I mean. But I think it's—important," she finished lamely.

Tip looked at her as if for the very first time he were really seeing only Corry Tipson, and not some Cordelia-Corry out of his own head.

"I like history," he said slowly. "But I never thought about. . . ."

"Vet, historian, housewife—" Gail ticked them off on her fingers. "Or housewife and maybe real-estate agent. I think I'd kind of like going around seeing all sorts of people's houses. That leaves you, Corry. So far computer programmer and accountant and pastry cook are out. So what is it now? Still a doctor's office?"

"I went to the library last week," Corry said slowly. "I looked up places where you can study ceramic art. There are lots, but no place really close. You can go to Ohio State, or Ohio University over at Athens, but they're so *big*. The book about colleges in the library is about twenty years old, and even way back then there were more than forty thousand students at Ohio State. I'd be scared spitless. You know I would."

"Doesn't any place smaller teach ceramics?" Don asked.

Corry shrugged. "There's the Cleveland Institute of Art. It's supposed to be really good, and you only have to be—or anyway *used* to have to be—in the upper fifty percent of your high school class. But it only took six hundred students, so it'd probably be hard to get into. Besides, the tuition was almost a thousand dollars. It'd be horriferous by now, and since I'd have to live away from home, it would cost even more still. So forget it."

"You ought to talk to Mrs. Eckert about it," Gail said firmly. "There might be scholarships or loans or whatever."

Corry didn't answer for a moment. Then, abruptly, she said, "I wrote to them. I know what Mom'll say, but I figured it wouldn't hurt to find out how much it'd cost. Maybe I could work for a year first to save up some money. Maybe even in one of the potteries. And maybe afterward be a designer for a pottery somewheres. I could still have my own studio and do my stuff. I've got all these ideas for. . . ."

The more excited she grew, gesturing, drawing in the air with her slender hands as she described the shapes and colors of imagined pieces, the more Tip's look of wonder, affection, and—almost—of envy deepened. But then, suddenly, she ran out of steam.

"It's probably all pie in the sky, like Mom says." She gave a nervous little shrug. "I don't know."

Tip looked at his watch and rose to cross to the kiln. Opening the peephole cover, he peered in, squinting against the glare.

There, glowing incandescent at the kiln's center, a chalice made of light, was old Lucas Henry's love-gift to Cordelia, remembered and made whole again through Corry's stubbornness and her skill.

Her gifts.

"*I* know," he said.

Author's Note

THERE REALLY WAS a Joshua Poole, and his pocket note-book and the 1891 bone-china formula really exist, but I have given it in *The Lotus Cup* to George Hankins who, like everyone else in the story, is my own invention. But though the characters are fictional, East Liverpool is real. I was born there, and though when I was ten my parents and sister and brother and I moved away from "The Hilltop," the cluster of family homes on what had once been Great-Grandpa's farm, I have been back often—once, briefly, to teach art at the old, now vanished, Central School on Fourth Street—and still have many ties there.

The town's Museum of Ceramics, run by the Ohio Historical Society, is a treasure, and owns a large collection of Lotus Ware, including the first piece I ever saw (and knew what I was seeing)—before the Museum was more than a gleam in William Vodrey's eye. From the evening in 1970 when he took that bowl from his mantel to show me,

I knew that one day I would write a story called *The Lotus Cup*. For years I had only the title, but then the story began to grow. Now that it is written I find myself envying Corry her project and her skill. My own grandfather was a pottery man and my father the best of ceramic engineers, and my mother has always kept a crock of clay on hand in case the urge to shape some new figure comes over her, but my own pieces have always been, to my mind, sadly lumpish. And so I have made my Lotus Cup with words instead.